"Perhaps the finest Irish novelist of his generation."

Robert McLiam Wilson

Maurice Leitch was born in 1933 and grew up in Northern Ireland. He worked as a teacher before joining the BBC as a features producer. In 1970 he moved to London where he produced radio drama for the BBC and he became editor of *A Book at Bedtime* on Radio Four in 1977 before becoming a full-time writer in 1989.

Maurice Leitch won the Whitbread Prize in 1981 for *Silver's City* and is also the author of *Poor Lazarus* (which was awarded the Guardian Fiction Prize in 1969) and *Seeking Mr Hare*.

In 1999 Maurice Leitch was awarded an MBE for services to literature.

GONE TO EARTH

Maurice Leitch

Maurice Leitch

turnpike
books

Copyright © 2019 by Maurice Leitch

First published by Turnpike Books

turnpikebooks@gmail.com

ISBN 9780993591365

Typeset by M Rules

Printed and bound by Clays Ltd, Elcograf S.p.A.

"Even if they hide beneath the earth, I shall dig them out; even if they are already dead, I shall kill them again."

GENERAL GONZALO
QUEIPO DE LLANO

ADRIANA

Leaving the house in the dark, as quietly as always, she makes her way up along Calle Agua then on past the church with the lion-jawed water-spouts where the women wash their clothes and gossip, although she trusts her own dirty linen's no longer of interest to them there. Silent on her feet as a ghost, she's wearing *alpargatos,* and remembers people during the "hunger years" fastening horseshoes to the soles to make them last longer. Now only the poor or very old in the *barrio* are seen with such things. Or someone with reasons of her own to creep along hugging walls.

Yet this night luck has deserted her, for on the outskirts of the pueblo she makes out twin pin-pricks of red in the shadows ahead. The two Civil Guards standing smoking there, waiting until she walks past before the younger one calls on her to halt, and heart pounding, she stops as they stroll towards her.

She knows them by sight as well as they know her, but the

1

one nicknamed the Toothpick is determined to have his sport, demanding, "What's in the bag? A *pistola,* is it? Or maybe a knife to slit some *falangist's* throat?" being well informed about the history of the man she's left sleeping back in their bed.

"Let's have a look at what you've got in there."

Taking her bag from her, he empties it on the ground while the other Guard shines his flashlight on the contents, her uniform of dark grey wool, plain black stockings and a pair of leather shoes which the younger one holds up.

"So where did you steal these from, eh?"

But the older one with the moustache tells him, "The senora works in the big new hotel below on the *costa*, let her pass."

Still feeling the urge to humiliate, Toothpick calls after her, "Only whores and *insurrectos* venture abroad at this hour!" Both torches staying trained on her until she reaches the cover of the cane-fields where the cicadas fall silent at her approach, as certain of her neighbours still do. There, they view the world through the eye of a needle, as someone has said of them. Which may well have been Diego himself, seeing more of life through that secret peep-hole of his than most of those passing by in the street below.

This path through the *campo* is something she's as familiar with as her own right hand by now. Only the seasons change, along with the crops. In winter the bare stalks rustle tinder dry and then fires are lit to clear the ground for the coming year's growth, and so she must go by road which means leaving the house even earlier, and thinking of the man above still snug and warm in their bed has her feeling sorry for herself.

Still, she knows not to dwell on something like that, tuning her ear instead to a familiar liquid sound, a secret she shares with the old man with his little garden kept verdant with water stolen from Don Fabio. When she comes up he bows as though acknowledging something illicit they have in common as now there are water-guards, like the other patrols stopping people from gathering esparto grass. As someone has said, truly General Franco is a great man, for he is teaching us Spaniards how to live without eating.

In his tiny oasis in the middle of the cane-fields the old man sits on a broken chair while the "borrowed" water refreshes his tomato crop. He also grows melons, eggplant, pimentos, and sometimes when she returns from her work he leaves out a bowl of them which she tips into her bag before walking on. Yet they never speak, and she wonders does he know about her husband, and is the widow of a *rojo* as bad as breaching a landowner's irrigation channel. So, one dark morning if she no longer hears that gentle trickle, coming across a patch of parched earth and a razed shack, her own luck may have also run out like her silent old ally's.

In the bad years when there was no work, and the men, white as the walls with hunger, stuck to the sides of the houses like flies, she and her mother would walk the thirty kilometres to Malaga to sell eggs, so this daily journey of hers is of no great consequence. In fact, she takes pleasure in being free for a time from the dread of someone knocking on the door to search the house. All it takes is one old enemy and a couple of witnesses to denounce Diego at the town hall.

Even so, may Dios forgive her, there are times when she wishes he never returned from the war to hide himself away in that tiny cupboard of a room of his, until an image of him

3

splayed and broken in a pit, or flung at the bottom of a well, enters her head, and she's glad he's come back to her.

Up ahead a glow in the sky comes from the lights of the hotel, the salty tang of the sea arriving as a shock, foreign, somehow, like that invisible continent out there in the dark. She can still distinguish that one wavering speck which Diego told her came from the one solitary street-lamp that Moroccan village could afford. After he was elected mayor, the only republican official the village had ever known, the work seemed never-ending, yet there were times when they could snatch a few hours together sitting here, staring out at that unseen land where a year later the red and gold banners of the Legion would be raised and their lives changed forever.

During daylight this expanse of shore stretches as far as the horizon itself, broken only by the great new hotel rising up like a blunt marble-clad finger of stone and glass for the foreign rich and famous requiring a hundred staff for their needs. She, Adriana, has been fortunate enough in finding work there despite Don Gustavo, the manager and a *madrileno*, despising the lazy donkey South. Having impressed him, however, she's now in charge of the care, cleaning and upkeep of four entire floors.

Directly in front of her is a grove of imported palm trees, and getting closer she hears the sound of a guitar, then a harsh voice singing, a *gitano's*, plainly, and sees a group of them sprawled on the ground with a bottle being passed around. Even in the near-dark, they seem drunk, one of them greeting her with a mocking, "Buenas noches, senora, out all alone by herself enjoying the night sea air."

4

Ignoring them, just as they would, too, have done if the *vino* hadn't been making them bold, she hears a very different voice break in. Clutching a bottle to his chest, a figure rises up, and she recognises this crazy, dancing, singing individual, for it's the famous Americano from the hotel everyone calls Senor Johnnie here with this trio of human jackals, one of whom joins him, fingers clicking, his friends encouraging him with yells and cries of street filth, which unlike the foreigner she understands only too well.

Spinning, whirling, voice slowing, he falls to the ground, greeted by mocking cries of, "*Hombre! Hombre!*"

As the sky's far lighter now she can see their faces for the first time, smell them, too, sour wine, tobacco, sweat, while the Americano lies flat on his back, the sight of that expensive pale suit of his on the dark soil a greater cause of concern about its future laundering than any present danger.

Confronting the bearded *gitano*, she tells him, "This foreign gentleman is a guest of the hotel where I'm employed so I must insist he now accompanies me there," all of it emerging as if from someone much more skilled at lying than herself.

"While the senor remains in our company, senora, you have my solemn word he will come to no harm."

Catching him glance at the Americano's expensive wrist-watch then his equally fine tan leather shoes, she says, "All I need do is call on the two *guardia* near by and allow them to resolve the matter."

"Senora, we are merely poor ignorant folk socialising with a fellow musician, but if it is your wish to escort him back to his hotel go with our blessing."

Taking hold of the Americano by both arms, she lifts him

to his feet, and although his eyes are closed he seems to be recovering some use of his limbs, mumbling, "mucho vino, clouding the brain, weakening the legs", in surprisingly good Spanish for a foreigner.

Although hauling a drunk man off to his bed is something she's only ever seen other women do, and even though darkness is on her side, what if someone sees her and carries the news back to Don Gustavo? Still, she has her own key to the kitchens at the rear of the hotel, and holding up the Americano she reaches the sanctuary of that familiar wooden door, turning the key in the lock while praying he won't fall asleep on her.

Deep in the underground *cocina* where Carlotta the cook rules, the only glimmer of light is from a Madonna votive lamp high on one wall, and that illuminated oval face looking down on her makes her even more determined to rid herself of her human burden. However, dragging him up four concrete flights in his present state is beyond her, so only the one alternative remains, the front elevators, except that out there Anselmo the night porter will be on duty.

The reception desk's almost forty feet away, and still hugging the Americano close to her she peers through the glass panel in the service door. The desk looks unattended, but Anselmo she's heard sometimes takes a nap when paid to be awake, so she hesitates, while, head falling forward on to his chest, the one she's propping upright mumbles something.

"Senor, senor," she whispers, "we must take the *ascensor*."

But she can see it's hopeless, his eyes closing again, accompanied by the sound of a first snore.

Placing a hand over his mouth, she propels him ahead of her

into the empty vestibule, looking towards the front desk where still nothing stirs, and reaching the elevators, she presses the nearest button. No light appears, however, and panic growing, clutching him, she stabs the remaining two before finally a bulb glows red. A six flashes, then five, four, three, two, one, until, cruelly, *bajo*, basement, stays lit.

At this point there's a distraction, the sound of a bell. Out there, some latecomer, face pressed to the glass, is anxious to get to his bed, his next ring more insistent, until a familar voice is heard complaining, "*Momento, senor, momentito, por favor!*" But before Anselmo's bald dome rises above the desk, another *ping* arrives, the elevator's doors sliding apart, and thrusting the Americano forward, she presses four.

Inside the mirrored compartment lingers the reek of a cigar, making her think of when the smoker was last here, and when the lift stops with a jolt the Americano slumps to the floor with her holding the doors open then lifting him to his feet and manoeuvring him out into the corridor beyond.

Reaching room four-0-four, unlocking the door with her master key, she pushes him inside. The interior's pitch black, but being familiar with the position of the bed, like every other one on this floor, steering him towards it, she fells him on top of the covers.

And so with him now safely stretched out there, her ordeal this night is finally over, even though standing listening to his breathing in the dark she knows she can never tell another living soul of this. Like the one now sleeping, it must remain her secret, hers, and the Americano's both.

JOHNNIE

The standing arrangement with reception is for them to buzz the room then ring back up at regular intervals until the phone gets answered, keeping on God knows how long. But then Senor Ray happens to be a famous American *cantante* who takes his rest in his own good time and it's an honour to have him staying with us here at the Miramar.

However, this time round, their persistence below seems to have paid off, and groaning, feeling about in the dark, he fumbles for the receiver.

"Senor? Senor Ray?" murmurs the voice on the other end, Don Gustavo himself, last thing Senor Ray needs right now with his waking dread of something with bared teeth ready to spring out at him even if it is only from the mouthpiece of a handset.

"Yeah?" and there it is again, same faraway tones enquiring, "Senor Ray?" until, finally, "A Senor Lang calling. Person to person. New York."

Don Gustavo's English sounds like he's learned it off one of those Speak Another Language In Twenty Easy Lessons tapes, and just to ruffle his feathers he sometimes calls him Gus for no other reason than he treats the staff like they're just off the farm, which most of them are, he imagines, just like himself once upon a time, this backwoods rube from Hopewell, Oregon, shit still on his shoes, only now they're four-hundred dollar, hand-stitched Weejuns.

"Tell him I'll ring back."

"You prefer him to ring *you*, Senor Ray?"

"No, no, tell him, tell him ..."

But his skull's starting to pound, and the phone falls back in its cradle.

Although he can't see it, a table-lamp's about a foot away, but he needs more time before allowing the merest sliver of light to enter the curtained-off room. Even without his hearing-aid, which he never wears in bed anyway, this other sound broaches the silence, some kind of pulsing flutter, and feeling a breeze on his face he realises it's the overhead fan, again something he invariably switches off.

Not feeling up to any sort of detective work right now, he lies there gauging the ferocity of his hangover on a scale of zero up to ten. Judging by first impressions this son-of-a-bitch might well hit double digits, but bringing it down to a more manageable figure are some lifesavers on the bureau, a bottle of Smirnoff, and his stash of "jelly beans".

Before popping one of those little green ovals he has to switch on the light. Anticipating that first searing shock to the eyeballs, he clicks it on, only then realising he's fully-clothed. Well, almost, for no socks, no shoes, and both soles

9

feel gritty, possibly sandy. So just where the heck has he been to end up spread-eagled like he's been dropped from a frigging helicopter?

Carefully rolling out of bed, he gauges the distance to the bureau, like he's done in a hundred other hotel bedrooms, and hands outstretched, he moves towards it. No time for the niceties of a glass, ice, neither, and twisting off the metal screw cap of the bottle, he takes that first bracer of the day prior to popping the pill.

Next, shuffling to the bathroom to check out the extent of the damage, suddenly this hobo in a wrecked six hundred dollar suit stares back at him from the mirror. But, worse, oh, a lot worse, down one cheek runs a line of scratch marks along with a livid patch of raw skin in the dead centre of his forehead.

Has he been involved then in some kind of maul or shindig? Certainly wouldn't be a first, other men's wives, girlfriends, etcetera, throwing themselves at him, and not just for an autograph, either, although that's mainly in the past, despite his Spanish fans still having the hots for Senor Emocion, The Nabob Of Sob, Prince Of Wails, or any of those other labels the press have hung on him.

"But what you wanna 'em to write?" his manager Bernie Lang's take on things. *"Perry Como's fans don't go round wrecking theaters, tearing up seats. Andy Williams', neither. Nor Frank's. But yours still do, and you go on selling records because of it. Right?"*

The phone rings again and unable to put it off any longer, he presses the receiver to his good ear, and it actually *is* Bernie on the line, sounding like he's ringing from Mars instead of mid-town Manhattan.

10

Before he can get a syllable out, his manager goes into instant Jewish attack mode.

"So why the fuck aren't you answering my calls? Know how much this is costing me? A goddam fortune, that's what. Where have you been, anyway? Don't tell me you're back on the sauce again."

"Bernie, this line is real bad," he manages to croak. "Can you call me back?"

"There's a fucking seven hours time difference, or are you on your own personal clock as usual?"

Then, "Don't you fucking hang up on me, you hear? Don't try that switching off the hearing-aid routine. Or the batteries are low. Fuck all that."

"I'm not wearing it."

"Well, put it the fuck back on. Losing my voice, as well as my patience here."

Glancing around, he searches for that familiar little earpiece and its trailing connection, but there's no sign of it.

"Okay, it's on again," he says, lying, and Bernie resumes his tirade, amidst all that transatlantic static something getting through about the forthcoming *Noche de Estrellas* booking.

"Don't go screwing this one up, you hear? If everything pans out we'll be able to extend the tour and take in London and 'Talk Of The Town'."

Then there follows something he has no wish to hear.

"How about I fly out, provide some moral support?"

"No, no, everything's fine here," he manages to mumble. "*I'm* fine," despite feeling a long way from it right now.

Perched on the edge of the bed he allows his gaze to travel, searching for the object which, weirdly enough, has become a trademark almost like it's grafted on. Fitted with his first model at fourteen, a Belmont Sonic, it was this heavy beige creation giving out squawks and squeals of feedback if the ear-piece wasn't connected properly. But who cared, he'd got the world back, the world before his stupid accident, everything returning in a rush of the most ordinary things, the sound of rain on a roof, crickets in a corn field, best of all, music. Music from that old portable Victrola he and his sister would lug out to the woods together. Up until then he'd lie in front of the radio, ear pressed to the speaker, which first alerted his folks to the problem. *Poor kid, he must be hard of hearing*, they'd whisper, enraging him, driving him deeper into his own head.

But all of that took place a long time ago, half a world away, and here and now starting to feel the first creeping progress of the downer, the earpiece must have fallen down alongside the bed somewhere, he reassures himself.

Lying back he stares up at the fan in the ceiling still lazily revolving, feeling himself slide back into a doze.

When he comes to, he forms the impression it must be late, but how late he can't be certain for now his watch is also missing. The water in the shower, as usual, takes aeons to heat, something the hotel promises to fix but never gets round to, but not wishing to come across as yet another complaining Americano ass-hole he's given up mentioning it. At least the flow is strong, and he stands in the stream letting its rush return him to some version of normality, responsibility, even, for what was it Bernie said about that next big concert? Barcelona, was it? Madrid?

Steering a razor around the abrasions on his face brings an

12

even more bracing touch of reality with finally some reasonable facsimile of the old Johnnie staring back at him. A layer of pancake base masks the very worst of the damage, and going back into the bedroom he picks out a pair of tan slacks and a cream-colored polo shirt.

A last minute pick-me-up from his bottle of Russian hooch, and he heads for the door, noticing the Do Not Disturb sign's missing, unless, of course, it's on the outside. But if he remembered to take care of something as automatic as that, what about the earpiece and the watch, billfold, as well, for that too is nowhere to be seen.

There's a safe in the room, so could the missing items be inside locked away along with his passport and travellers' cheques? All he has to do is punch in some numbers. But what in god's name are they? The thing itself is set in the wall by the window, and going down in front of it like it's some kinda shrine, and praying for a miracle of sorts, he taps out, ten, one, two, seven, his birth date, which has got to make sense, right?

But nothing happens, *nada*. Still, down on the front desk they must have their own combination for such emergencies, and he's about to get up off his knees when the phone rings again. Instead of going silent after the stipulated half dozen, however, it continues to buzz, until unable to stand it any longer, lifting the receiver, he hears a familiar voice announce, "I'm pleased to report, Senor Ray, your missing property has been retrieved and can now be collected below at your earliest convenience."

Then a long pause.

"Senor Ray, Senor Ray, can you hear me?"

But this is no time for irony, for Don Gustavo is his best

buddy now, his bearer of good news, and he should be grateful, which he is, and will make certain to make it up to him because of it.

"Can you send someone up to the room with them?"

This time there's a longer hesitation, and jamming the receiver closer to his ear, he asks, "Is there some kind of problem?"

"No, no, no *problema*, Senor Ray, the items are here for you as we speak. But the *policia* would very much appreciate if you could come down and collect them in person."

"Police?"

"Si, Capitano Delgado wishes to speak with you directly regarding the recovery of the items."

Suddenly another drink plus another M&M seems a good idea.

"Very well, inform the captain I'll be down presently."

"But, of course, Senor Ray. I will tell him, Senor Ray. Thank you, Senor Ray."

Going down in the elevator he still feels jittery, that word *policia,* no matter what the language, something to worry about. When the ground floor doors slide open, Don Gustavo, or Gus, as he's decided to re-name him because of the creepy way he's acting in front of the police captain, more like a military general than any cop he's ever seen, starts babbling, "Senor Ray, Senor Ray, Capitan Delgado has your valuables and it will now be his privilege to return them to you."

All this time, Capitan Delgado, smoking one of those long thin black cheroot things, has been leaning on the desk in that casual, yet coiled up way cops cultivate the world over. Dark, good-looking, oiled hair. Until suddenly the handsome features relax and, smiling, he advances with outstretched hand.

"Senor Ray, accept my apologies for this grave inconvenience whilst a guest in our country. Be assured those responsible are already in custody and will pay dearly for bringing disgrace to our reputation for hospitality towards all our foreign friends, especially one as famous as yourself."

Not only does the guy not talk like a cop, he doesn't smell like one either, his cologne eclipsing his own Aqua Velva.

"But, forgive my poor manners, here are the items in question," taking out the Rolex and bill-fold and handing them over.

"In the *billeteria* we found your American driving license and identification papers. Still, if I may be so bold to enquire, had you also a sum of money in the *billeteria*?"

Incapable of remembering any of it, Johnnie shakes his head.

"These *cabron* might have got away claiming the *dinero* as their own, but the watch was another matter, which is why our guardia colleagues became suspicious."

Already his head is over-loaded with too much information, most of it irrelevant, for the million dollar question remains, where's the fucking hearing-aid? Finally, when he comes out with it, the captain looks confused until Don Gustavo explains, "Senor Ray employs an *audiofono*," and after a pause, the cop says, "In that case I suggest Senor Ray waits here in the bar until my men and I continue our interrogation."

A rapid formal bow and off he goes leaving him standing there, Don Gustavo telling one of the busboys to serve him with whatever he'd like on the house. The kid, a tall, gangly teenager in his grey and navy uniform leads the way to the lounge decorated with framed portraits of the hotel's illustrious showbiz visitors, Sophia Loren, Sean Connery, Rudolf Nureyev and, of course, Ava Gardner with that fuck Sinatra. He's been promised a spot up there himself, but he's not holding his breath.

Without a word young Jorge the cocktail waiter mixes him a stiff vodka tonic as though recognising the need for something potent, even if it is only four-thirty in the afternoon by the watch now back on his wrist. The ice cubes in the tall glass make contact with his teeth, then that first long, delicious swallow, and without needing to be told Jorge sets him up another.

Late at night, just the pair of them in the place, he and the kid have the sort of one to one drinkers have in hotel bars everywhere. Like all the waiters, the kid's ravenous for anything to do with America, so he tells him about himself and his life there when they were the same age, and leaning across the kid hangs on every word, and it's always the same version, shaped and refined over the years, even if this is only some poor kid from the *barrio* and not someone from the papers or a fan club.

He's been doing it too long to change the routine now. The Boy Scout camp blanket toss at fourteen, landing on the ground with a straw piercing his right eardrum, then all the other stuff, playing the organ in church, taking off to make his mark in LA. and the hard times trudging from agency to agency with cardboard in his shoes before the first real spot in a black R & B joint in South Central playing piano and singing.

Jorge's eyes light up the way his own once did listening to some old pro in some upholstered sewer on the club circuit. *Show-business, kid? Ever played two weeks in Ashtabula, Ohio?* Actually, he had.

Whatever's going down at the police car lasts roughly the time it takes to have another vodka tonic, so when the cop returns he's feeling decidedly more chipper. Sliding on to the stool alongside, the captain says, "Permit me to join you, senor?" then, "*Conac*, por favor, " Jorge reaching for a bottle of Courvoisier before moving discreetly out of earshot to the far end of the bar.

"Your good health, Senor Ray, and may the remainder of your stay with us here turn out to be a happier one."

Raising glasses, they drink, and after a time the cop takes out a cigarette case, offering it, but in no mood for one of those skinny black things Johnnie shakes his head and Delgado lights up, his lighter also silver with a crest.

"The *cabron* out in the car claims you made him a gift of the watch, in addition to the money. He also insists he knows nothing about any *audiofono*, even what such an object is, or even looks like. But lying comes as natural as breathing to such scum. To treat them as equals is a mistake. After the bad years, thanks to the Generalissimo we're now able to enjoy *la vida dulce* while remaining ever vigilant against those who would seek to spoil it for the rest of us."

Jorge, already hovering with fresh glasses, directs a nervous glance at the Franco portrait on the far wall. Observing the young kid, it strikes Johnnie why didn't he ask him if he'd been in the place last night and if so what might have taken place. But does he really wish to find out? Still, knowing cops, and this one seems no different despite the fancy talk, he realises he won't let the matter drop even after returning his watch and wallet. Already he's lowered the equivalent of three treble brandies while *he* is getting more sober.

Easing himself down off his stool, the captain excuses himself, making for the can, while he and Jorge watch. Finally, the kid breaks the silence.

"Forgive me for saying this, but not everyone is your friend here, Senor Ray. Certain people, as we sometimes say, have the two faces, one for the street, and one for behind the door," and just when there seemed there might be more of the same, he closes down, and after Delgado returns in a cloud of cologne the kid takes himself off to the business end of the bar as though he's said more than he should.

"Come, *amigo*, let's you and I go and see if those lying sons of gipsy whores have the *cojones* to look you in the face or not."

Definitely tipsy now, riding boots planted wide apart, he has this wild look in his eye, more worryingly, his revolver holster flap's unbuttoned, and without settling up, but then when did cops ever pay a tab anywhere, he makes for the door.

Outside the two civil guards are leaning against the car smoking. Seeing their superior approach they quickly throw their butts away, salute, then start hauling the prisoner from the back seat of the vehicle. The gipsy's handcuffed, his gaze fixed on the ground, but when Delgado says something to him he lifts his head to stare at Johnnie.

The *gitano*, as they call him, is wearing filthy torn jeans and

18

a buttoned up plaid shirt. When he opens his mouth there's a flash of gold, and even though he's swarthy as hell his face looks like it's taken a real pasting with one eye closed.

"Is this man familiar to you, senor? He persists in saying he met with you last night."

Delgado's watching him closely, making him nervous and so, jumping in, he says, "Could you ask him again about the hearing-aid?"

Coming up close, Delgado lays a hand on the guy's bearded cheek, almost caressing it in some creepy way, and they begin talking quietly together.

"What's he saying?"

Delgado shrugs.

"Much as before. It's my opinion he knows nothing about the item in question. Still, now that we're here, let's you and I take a little *paseo* together."

He says something to the guards who grab hold of the prisoner, then start dragging him out of the hotel car-park.

"Where are they taking him?"

But the captain only grins.

"Come, you will see."

Setting out after them he realises they're heading towards the sea. Starting to stagger a little from the effects of the booze and having some sort of haze in front of his eyes he feels in no condition to offer any form of resistance, verbal, or otherwise, and finally reaching the *playa*, he ploughs on, shoes sinking in the soft sand.

This expanse of roped-off beach is the private domain of the hotel, the public section lying over to the left on the Torremolinos side. Homing in on a small clump of palm-trees about a hundred yards further on, and arriving there, those ahead wait for him and their captain to catch up, and when they do there's more of that same murmured one-to-one between Delgado and the prisoner.

The gypsy's pointing to the ground, then off somewhere among the trees, until in a sudden shocking turn-around Delgado pulls out his revolver and the prisoner falls to his knees, the gun pointing at his head, one of the guards coming forward with his truncheon in his hand.

It's this real nightmare scenario, something he feels he may have somehow set off himself, thinking, surely this is a little extreme for just a fucking robbery. Then, again, was it *really* one?

The second guard, the older one with the Jerry Colonna moustache, is signalling frantically now, and very slowly the captain lowers the pistol. Over by one of the palm trees the same guard's holding up something in his hand. By the dangling wire Johnnie can tell it's the missing Belmont Sonic, and when the cop brings it over Delgado inspects it as if it's this crucial piece of evidence.

"Is this your missing property, senor?" and when he tells him, yeah, that's correct, handing it to him, Delgado says, "In that case you're exceptionally lucky as these ignorant people might easily have thrown it into the sea and you might never have retrieved it."

All of them, even the gypsy kneeling on the ground, are looking at him now as though expecting a demonstration of some kind and so shaking it a little for effect he puts it to his left ear.

"If there's any way I can show my appreciation for the safe

return of this along with my watch and wallet, you and your men have only to ask."

Returning the compliment, the captain says, "Any small success we may have had in recovering the property of such a famous visitor, will, we hope, be some consolation for the regrettable experience you've suffered."

Already, however, he's had a belly-full of all of this verbal shimmying around, and even though he knows he shouldn't, he can't resist enquiring, "What going to happen to him? After this, I mean?"

"It's your statutory right to press charges, and if you decide to do so he will end up in one of our Malaguena prisons."

"Well, seeing as all my belongings have been safely restored to me, I'm perfectly happy to let the matter end right here and now."

"You have a tender and forgiving heart like all Americanos, senor. Nevertheless, almost certainly, we will catch him again."

Expecting to see the handcuffs come off, he waits for the captain's order, but after a nod from Delgado the two guards haul the gypsy to his feet, frogmarching him back the way they'd come, and now the cop is grinning at him as though eager to impart something private just between the pair of them.

"Our *gitano amigo* says a female may have also been present last evening, and that you and she went back to the hotel together. Still, even if such a thing were true, a man's private business is solely his own concern. But, on a much more agreeable topic, I understand you will be performing in Torremolinos tomorrow evening, so perhaps we might meet up there again, but in less official circumstances this time."

21

This time the handshake is as firm and as warm as one could possibly hope for.

After the cop had gone, he stayed where he was among the palm trees trying to process everything he'd just seen and heard, but specifically and worryingly, the latter, for, a *woman*? *How, why, in God's name?*

Leaning against one of the ribbed trunks, he closes his eyes, but nothing illuminating appears behind the lids, only a blank flecked by a few blood-motes. When he opens them again, clipping the hearing-aid back on, the sudden roaring of the sea produces nothing likely to reassure him either.

DIEGO

Now that Adriana has found employment less of his time is spent braiding *esparto* for donkey panniers, bridles, mats, baskets, and those thatched beach cones the tourists lie under. Something he finds difficult to visualise, like so many other things that have passed him by, all those foreigners broiling in the sun, hell-bent on looking like field-hands and smelling of coconut oil, then, according to Adriana, getting it on the sheets and pillowcases, keeping the great washing machines in the bowels of the Miramar constantly thrumming.

So, these machines, what are they like, he asks, and how do they dry the clothes as well as clean them? Even enquiring about the company that makes them, German, naturally, and she looks at him wondering why such things should interest someone like him. But they do, determined on him not ending up like some dried up *pensionista*, nothing occupying his mind but that next plait of *esparto*.

At first the work helped stave off the boredom until he turned more and more to reading, then writing in the school exercise-books Adriana buys for him in Malaga. Already a sizeable stack thickens on the shelf alongside his radio, which every evening he tunes in to between seven and midnight, ear pressed to its gauze-covered speaker, the signal wavering as though blown off course by the winds travelling from Moscow or Paris, or across the sea from London, the Spanish services from those foreign stations his salvation and sanity for these twenty odd years.

With her first month's wages Adriana brought back the latest Grundig model, also German. When silent, it sits covered by a cloth like some sacred relic, for she's not as disapproving of the church as he is. Now, when he sees the young priest walking in the street below with his nose in his breviary, he remembers what happened to his predecessor and how he was powerless to stop it.

He'd been away on some union business that day, and when he got back a mob of anarchists had arrived in cars from Fuengirola, taking over the entire village. The militia men had locked themselves in their barracks, so the anarchists had the run of the place, driving up and down, yelling, "Death to *la gente gorda*, the fat people!" even though most of those had long since fled.

When he and his two UGT colleagues reached the plaza he recognised some of those waving flags and firing shotguns in the air, the sort only too happy to settle grudges against those they wouldn't normally dare face. One of them, a low-life *cabron* and petty thief from his own street, saw him getting out of the car and called out something to his new-found friends about the village being a nest of fascists needing burned out. Clearly drunk, he had an expensive looking straw hat on his head looted from the only outfitter's in the village where the well-off purchased their clothes. Staggering up to him, and sweeping off his brand new panama, he delivered an extravagant bow.

"As our first elected socialist mayor, Don Diego, why don't you do us the honour of lighting the pueblo's main bonfire of the day?"

Like almost everyone else there the drunk had a nick-name, *El Jaiba*, the Crab. Yet it wouldn't do to address him in that way. Certain customs never change, like the people themselves, a source of frustration when he himself had tried bringing in laws aimed at making their lives better.

"I see, Luis Casares, you've become one of those who wear their privilege on their heads when once you were another of the hat-less ones like all the rest of us."

That set him back on his heels, the laughter from those watching making his shame even worse, one of the men stand-ing outside The Sports Bar, declaring, "My old mule Pepe, he, too, wears a straw bonnet in the noonday heat," provoking an even greater cry of derision.

After the Crab had slunk off, leaving his new headgear lying in the gutter, nothing could defuse the violence. The anarchists turned their fury on the church, pulling down the holy pictures and statues, looting the more valuable relics, while with some of the older villagers he tried reasoning with them, telling them religion no longer had any power now the republic was in place. But they wouldn't be persuaded, pointing their guns at them, the women in black weeping, crossing themselves.

Their leader was a sharecropper by the name of Gonzalez who'd lost his livelihood when the rich *senorito* who owned his land had thrown him and his family off their tiny holding. Now he directed his men to the one place where those known to be on the side of the *falangists* could be found, crying, "Where's the priest? Where's Father Gregorio? Bring him out!" The priest was hiding up in the bell-tower and it looked as though he would be cast down and dashed at our feet but, instead, Gonzalez paraded him through the streets with a horse's bridle about his neck, blaspheming him, forcing him to drink vinegar, before dispatching him with a bullet in the back of the head at the village rubbish dump.

A black day for everyone, that was, and when the fascists regained control they made certain of retribution, just like they continue to do, and why he remains hidden in his own home like some silent ghost living in constant fear of discovery.

Every so often, however, a marriage procession fills the street, and with his eye pressed to the hole in his curtain he feasts on the faces below, trying to put names to as many as he can, although if the guests are the same age as the bride and groom he can only hazard a guess. Parents and older relatives are easier to recognise, although he's shocked at how old they've become. But then the mirror in his room is either a good liar or a generously forgiving one, the face staring back at him from the glass having barely changed as he sees it.

In the middle of June, hearing the church bells ring out, he gets ready behind the curtain, waiting for the procession to appear. Already the women of the street are out on their doorsteps, so it's a bonus to observe those who knew him when he was their neighbour.

There's Senora Ramirez and her daughter Maria Concepta who'd once been the village beauty, but now looking like her own mother, and the Gomez twins in black, funerals always being more to their taste. Casting his gaze along the line of wives, grandmothers and aunts with folded arms, he thinks of Adriana and how when he crept back like a thief in the night he'd made her a widow, too, in name, if not in reality. Then he remembers how she never cared all that much for the close embrace of that sisterhood anyway.

Now can be heard a growing hum of voices accompanied by the screeching of a small band, so he realises this is no ordinary *barrio* wedding. Looking down on the heads below, he spots a scattering of dress uniforms, military, as well as *guardia civil,* imagining the scent of pomade and cologne rising up from those parading there.

All have their eyes fixed on the person in front, as just here the street's at its narrowest, except for one person, that is, looking up, not at the sky, but the houses opposite, as is his companion, this foreign-looking *rubio* in a white suit. Stepping aside together, they're gazing directly up at his own window now, the sudden shock pulling him back from the curtain and into the room again until the sound of the band has completely faded away. Then, kneeling there, he brings his eye up close to the glass, but the street's deserted, even the doorstep women having all gone inside.

After a time he opens a book but can't concentrate. Taking off his glasses, instead he stares at the wall, unable to stop thinking of the pair staring up at his window. Even though it's not the first time someone has lingered outside, these two seemed different, particularly the foreigner with his blond hair and sun-scorched face like one of the tourists from Adriana's hotel.

As for the second man, he feels certain he was Spanish, even though he had been unable to get a look at his face. Yet something in the way he carried himself, he felt he recognised, some tell-tale tilt and twist of his torso under that expensive jacket singling him out from all those others in the procession.

The rest of the day the episode still haunts him, a memory of some *one* hovering there just beyond recall, and when the late afternoon produces the first trickle of returning wedding guests he goes back to his place at the window. Wine's been drunk, there's shouting and laughter, the young men following hot on the heels of the girls holding on to one another advancing in a giggling line down the middle of the street.

Later, at dusk, the lights in the trees in the plaza will come on, the signal for the *paseo* to begin. Even *he* knows that will never change, recalling the evening he first saw Adriana in her ruffled dress walking with her two plain cousins and was smitten with a kind of fever, clammy palms, dry tongue, even though he already had a reputation for being good with words, having taught himself to read and write after work in his father's barber's shop on Calle Isidoro. Now, hearing the cries of the young, he imagines he, too, is down there himself invisible in the shadows, shocked at seeing so much change, for even though many of those sitting outside the cafes are his contemporaries *they* hadn't been frozen in a twenty-year old block of ice as he has.

*

When Adriana came home they sat facing one another across their small table eating together in silence. After another long day tending to those with too much wealth and leisure to care who was cleaning after them, she was tired, although not all were like that, she told him, the Germans even making their own beds. But then that was their mentality, he said, as methodical in someone else's country in their own domestic habits as dropping their bombs on Guernica, Malaga or Madrid.

Still, this evening he wishes to steer any conversation towards more local matters, casually enquiring if she'd come across any of the party from today's wedding still in the square, until she reminds him she never takes that route any longer. Yet even at the risk of kindling her suspicions, he returns to the procession passing the house that afternoon.

Luckily she laughs, telling him he's getting as bad as his nosey old lady neighbours, and so treading almost as carefully as he pads overhead, he remarks, "Somehow I don't think they were from the barrio. The ones getting married, I mean."

"And why do you say that?"

"Well, money. The look, the smell of it."

Again she laughs. "Somebody's nose has certainly got sharp, even behind glass."

"One was a foreigner. Older, reddish-blond hair, face of a drinker. And, yes, with a limp," recalling his gait when he and his companion moved off together.

"Like the Crab, you mean? My, but you wouldn't recognise him for the swell he's become."

On the table is a carafe of wine, and in a sort of rush, filling his glass, he drinks it straight down.

"Is your stomach troubling you again?" she asks, for there have been times when he's had some problems in that area, and he's feeling his insides clench once more, knowing now who that second stranger was, with that scuttling walk of his, branding him with his nickname, *El Jaiba,* the Crab.

After Adriana had gone to bed, he pulls his chair close to the wireless to listen to the familiar voice of Jorge Olivar on Radio Moscow, and even though the headline bulletin is the shooting down of Gary Powers' CIA spy-plane and his capture by the Soviets, he can't concentrate. Tuned to the low, confidential murmur of the famous exile's Castilian tones, it might as well be Chinese, for in his head he's hearing the brassy echo of a band of local wedding musicians, and closing his eyes, two figures staring up at his curtained window, one a stranger, the other an old enemy with a long memory and an ancient grudge to settle.

EUGENE

Save for the one they call the *Americano,* the Hollywood Room's empty tonight, young Jorge the barman greeting him with a grin and a "*buenas noches, Senor Eugene,*" setting out whiskey and agua as for a regular. But then the bar serves as a stopping-off place before facing his apartment in Las Golondrinas where he might carry on with a bottle of his own if the mood calls for a final nightcap.

Normally he takes his place at the bar facing a faded Christmas calendar advertising schnapps, rosy-cheeked *kinder* in woolly hats throwing snowballs, reminding him, perhaps, of another wintry landscape not so very different from the one on the poster, even if the setting outside is as far removed from Leitrim as day is from night.

This evening, however, the only other patron has taken his spot, so he moves to the other end of the bar. He could, of course, have made his way to one of the club chairs at a corner

31

table overlooked by a smouldering Ava Gardner and a shark-ishly smiling Frank Sinatra, but as long as he can remember he's been this one foot propped on a brass rail kind of drinker.

Scrupulous not to display any hint of favouritism, Jorge stands equidistant between his two customers, holding a tumbler up to the light, polishing it with a napkin, finally placing bowls of olives and peanuts in front of them, but no ash-trays, aware that neither is a smoker.

Gazing into space with nothing to be heard but the occasional clink of glass on glass and the soft flutter of the overhead fans, there they sit in a moment of boozy introspection, before noting the need for another, Jorge pours Furlong a second shot of John Jameson, neat, never ice, unlike his other patron whose highball glass is topped up with fresh cubes along with either gin or vodka by the look of it.

Like all the waiters in the hotel keen to practise their English, Jorge finally is the one breaking the silence.

"May I ask a favour of you, Senor Ray, to sign this?" to which the American replies, "Don't tell me it's the tab already. Surely you can trust me after all this time."

Clearly he's making fun of him, but, eyes widening in alarm, the young barman stammers, "No, no, not *la cuenta*, senor!" pushing forward something instead which the other barely glances at before asking, "Got a pen handy?"

Desperately searching for one, Jorge dives below the bar, until taking pity on him, Furlong offers, "Here, use this," uncapping his own old green Parker.

"Well, who do I make this out to? Yourself?" the singer asks, and Furlong sees it's a photograph, its glossy black and white surface reflecting the light.

"No, no, senor, my sister Maria Dolores," and laughing, the American scrawls a signature, then something else across the face on the photograph which Furlong recognises as his own.

After the pen's been returned to its owner, raising his glass, the singer says, "Seeing as both of us have this late night den of iniquity to ourselves, would you have any objection if I joined you?" Each word, each syllable weighed for maximum effect, making it obvious he's already pretty far gone, although not in any unpleasant, potentially combative way.

"Not in the slightest. Furlong's the name. Eugene Furlong."

"Ray, Johnnie, as in J-o-h-n-n-i-e, not the misspelt version on that *Los Tres Gatos* marquee in downtown Torremolinos."

Climbing on to the stool alongside him, the American asks, "Staying here in the hotel yourself?"

"No, just dropping in for one for the road."

"While keeping company with some of our stars of the silver screen?" pointing to the array of framed portraits lining the walls.

By some stroke of irony Furlong had himself been invited to see this Johnnie character perform this evening at a gala performance attended by a gathering of the most influential people here on the *costa*, the mayor, his wife, his daughters, but especially the womenfolk in a high state of excitement at getting to witness the famous crooner in the flesh. Guzman, an aquaintance of Furlong's, informing him that anyone who was anyone would be there.

"While you, my Irish *campadre*, might even renew acquaintance with some of your old comrades from the fifteenth *bandera*."

33

However, despite never being one for reunions, especially of the veterans sort, Furlong allowed Guzman squeeze a promise from him to turn up, and he *had* made his way to the venue at the heart of San Miguel, going into a bar there to prime himself in advance with a *rioja* or two.

Sitting by the window he could see eveything that was happening outside, *guardia* clearing the street for the arriving *ricos* in their limousines, a couple of British Bentleys and a white Rolls Royce among them, their doors swinging open and their women stepping out, many in furs even though the night was exceptionally balmy for the time of year.

Behind him he could hear the running commentary of the drinkers at the bar standing ankle-deep in the usual drift of sun-flower husks there. Once this had been a *rojos'* bar, and some residue of it lingered like the reek of black tobacco and spilt red wine, for his Spanish was good enough to make out what was being said, most of it filthy directed at what lay under all that perfumed mink and foreign silk outside. The men, also, coming in for derision of the sort that could earn one a bad beating plus a month or two in jail.

Dressed in his one good linen, lightweight summer suit, he knew they had him down as some harmless tourist who'd wandered in and soon would make his way out again, which suited him. Just another foreigner escaping from a past which was *his* business and no-one else's.

Watching the procession file past flanked by the *guardia* in their buttoned up uniforms and glazed leather tricorn hats, he imagined he, too, was seeing them with the same steely gaze of the drinkers at the bar in their work-hardened corduroy and blue overalls, faces dark as the *ricos'* women's were pale.

Helped on by the *rioja*, it was a moment of easy sentiment which wouldn't last he knew, yet it still contained an element of truth, remembering how there'd been a time when he'd hated his own home-grown *ricos* with *their* privilege and big houses, even taking part in burning some of those to the ground, until another voice in his head reminded him this was Spain, not Ireland, and a young twenty-two year old had himself once served under those same red and gold colours flying outside.

More and more cars were drawing up outside now, and at his back one of the drinkers remarked, "It's nice to see our betters out enjoying themselves, don't you think? Dressed to kill, isn't that the expression?"

"Along with our own brave boys in uniform taking time off from their barrio duties?"

"Speaking of the barrio, I saw Don Luis, as he now calls himself, turning up along with some of his rich new friends."

"Still, you know what they say about a leopard changing its spots? Or, in this case, something having crawled out of the sea."

Hearing Guzman openly mocked in this way gave Furlong an uneasy feeling, making the prospect of mingling with *El Jaiba*, the Crab and his fat cat friends later on something to avoid. Better to stay where he was, and going up to the bar he ordered *una otra copa, por favor,* and the owner, this big, fat-bellied *Andalus*, barely throwing him a glance, refilled his glass for him.

That was two, maybe three hours previously when the clock in his head told him it was still too early to go back to his lonely apartment. Strung along the beach below the town, however, were several *chiringuitos* still serving, and keeping to the side streets where only the cats and dogs nosed among the garbage he made his way down towards the sea. At this time of night he had the descent to himself, the only lighting coming from the moon and the reflected sheen of the sea, and despite the lure of someone in a pale suit out alone with a touch of unsteadiness in his gait, he had no fear of being waylaid. One thing the *Caudillo* had done was make it safe for people like Furlong abroad on their own like this.

After more drinks in Ramon's, then Enrique's, then Maria Rosario's, he'd finished up in the Miramar, meeting the Americano there and each time offering to pay for a round being met with, "Put it away, buddy, your money's no good here. Anyway, it's not often I get a chance to shoot the breeze with someone who speaks the same language. Begging your pardon, of course, young Jorge," who merely grinned.

"Might be surprised to learn I've some Irish in me myself. Dash of Blackfoot, too, but then stuff like that only fills column inches. Incidentally, don't suppose you caught my show in town tonight, did you?"

"Afraid not."

"Well, reckon you didn't miss much. Hardly the London Palladium, or the Paris Hippodrome."

He laughs.

"Jeez, some of the joints I've played. Two waiters, a drunk hooker and a dog. Even the pooch fell asleep. But, hey, here in sunny Spain some folk might still remember the name."

"*All* our people know your music, Senor Ray," Jorge chimes in, eyes wide with sincerity. "The Little White Cloud Who Cries"? My sister's favourite."

36

"Guess two million copies, numero uno, five weeks, can't be all that bad ... So, Irish, tell me, how'd you end up here far away from all those green fields and grey skies back home?"

"Just sort of drifted down this way."

"Yeah, wouldn't mind taking up some sorta residence here myself. Little *casa* beside the sea? Walks along the beach? Same set-up as your own, I imagine."

"Not really. Still waiting for that big lottery ticket to turn up like everybody else."

"Take it from somebody who's seen and done all that, runs away just like piss down a drain. Like this stuff right here in front of us, eh?"

Which unfortunately was the wrong thing to hear just then, Furlong's bladder responding in kind, and so leaving his drinking companion staring at the unseasonal calendar on the wall facing him, he heads for the *servicios*.

Making his way along the corridor to the jakes he's struck by the eerie sensation no-one's actually staying here, the silence, plus all the trapped air, muffling any clue to an other human presence. But then when a new place opens its doors here, the locals always flock to gape at the imported marble and mosaic floors, the commissioned mural in the dining-room by the famous Madrid artist, and when the novelty wears off it's left to only the foreign tourists to populate the place.

Each morning as he takes his stroll along the beach he can see them soaking up those already early tanning rays, while beyond the hotel's low perimeter wall the hawkers gaze hungrily in, although those same gypsy men and women never approach *him*. Perhaps it's because his one linen suit and ancient panama are showing signs of wear and tear a bit like himself, with Guzman constantly exhorting him to get someone in to do his washing, cleaning, cooking, too.

"With a touch of the old rumpy pumpy thrown in as well, eh? After all, you're still a red-blooded *hombre* with everything still in working order. At least, so I've been reliably informed," that gold-toothed grin of his saying it all regarding his occasional visits to Dona Dolores's establishment on Calle Los Nidos.

Back in the Hollywood Room there's been a development, two visitors having arrived, sprawled on adjoining stools at the bar as though the place belongs to them. One is Guzman, and his companion, that police captain friend of his, an opened bottle of champagne in front of them, and when Guzman sees him approaching he greets him with dismissive wave of the hand.

"Better late than never, I suppose, after not showing up for this gentleman's performance this evening. But we won't hold that against you, as neither will he, I imagine."

Senor Ray, however, appears a lot more drunk now than when he left him and is only capable of mustering a weak grin.

"But tell me, *amigo*, why do we find you here and not with your Spanish friends expecting you in Torremolinos? Could it have something to do with a certain senora, perhaps, whose past, let us say, leaned formerly more to the left than the right?"

Still, if Guzman was banking on impressing his policeman friend with his sarcasm he was due for a disappointment, Delgado growling, "Let's have some decent Spanish *conac* instead of this French piss so we can drink a toast to a *real* hero of the people and not these foreign *putas* soiling the walls," gesturing towards Franco's portrait among that other black and white gallery of celebrities.

"Why no *matadors?* No Manolete, no Ordonez, no Dominguin? No Olivares, no Santamaria?" naming a couple of Real footballers. "Did we not spill good Spanish blood to rid ourselves of this imported filth?"

He was glaring at Jorge as he spoke, Furlong, as well, but neither was prepared to risk offending such a thug, and when the brandy arrives, they, too, dutifully raise their glasses to his toast.

"Long live the Generalissimo! Viva Espana!"

"And may those who insult either or both end up in the same shit-hole!" cries Guzman.

Throughout all his the American has been staring into his glass. But now he speaks up.

"Those poor bastards who took my watch, did you let 'em go?"

But it's Guzman who answers and not his captain friend who's still glaring at the photographs on the wall.

"Those poor bastards, as you describe them, need taught a hard and painful lesson, otherwise they will continue robbing respectable people such as yourself."

The American laughs.

"A heck of a long time since anyone called me *that.*"

For some reason this appeared to enrage the captain, who suddenly pulled out his pistol, laying it on the bar in front of him, everyone freezing, until the singer drawls, "Last time I saw something like that coulda been in a Gene Autry movie."

"This is not the Wild West, senor. Although, is it true that

39

in certain parts of your country some of your compatriots put hoods over their heads like our own Easter *penitentos* and hang black people from trees?"

"Some of those same rednecks would quite happily string *me* up, too, given half a chance."

"And why would that be, given your own complexion is obviously more *rojo* than *negro?*"

During their verbal encounter the American has kept a smile on his face, but now he stares long and hard at his inquisitor, Guzman quickly breaking in, "We poor provincials don't often get the opportunity of seeing and hearing such an internationally acclaimed artist as yourself, Senor Ray, right here in our own back-yard, as you Americanos like to say. Isn't that the expression?"

"Enough of the Senor Ray, call me Johnnie."

After this there's a lull, the atmosphere reverting to some form of normality, save for the revolver still in full view on the bar, of course. Yet even that seemed to have lost its threat.

"Well, as you also like to say in both your own countries, time to call it a day," finally Guzman announces. "*Capitan*, shall you and I be on our way and leave these two gentlemen in peace?"

Reaching for his pistol and slipping it back in its holster, the captain slides from his stool, Guzman laying a steadying hand on his arm, and they walk to the door where outside Delgado's police car, a gleaming Italian Fiat, can be seen through the glass, Furlong wondering who'll be doing the driving. Not that anyone in a uniform here would dare challenge their superior of being drunk at the wheel.

After they've gone, Furlong felt like leaving himself, the man alongside him clearly no longer capable of carrying on a conversation, staring glassily ahead as though off into empty space.

"*La cuenta, por favor.*"

But Jorge shrugs, pointing towards the American, indicating he's already paid for them both. Even so, Furlong lays a ten peseta note on the bar, and the boy tells him, "I will make certain the senor gets back to his room. Here in the hotel we're all of us familiar with the senor's habits."

Outside, the Fiat still hasn't driven away, Furlong wondering why until he catches sight of its owner noisily sprinkling one of the shrubs near the hotel's entrance. There's no sign of Guzman, but as he makes to slip past in the darkness he hears him call out his name, realising he's in the driving seat with the window rolled down.

"Permit me to offer you a lift, *amigo?*"

"It's okay. I only live a short distance away."

"None the less, we both would like to talk with you. Come, get in, and sample the luxury of Italian upholstery for yourself."

And when he does slide into the rear seat, it does, indeed, smell of expensive new cowhide, as well as cologne and cigars.

Straight away Guzman puts it to him, "Just how well do you know our American *cantante* friend back there?"

"I only met him the first time this evening."

"Ah, so you say.."

There's a silence, Furlong wondering why it's taking Delgado this long to empty his bladder, unless, of course, it's to allow his sidekick time to interrogate him, for that's where this seems to be leading.

"Still, I suppose, it's perfectly understandable two people sharing the same language, becoming *intimo*, shall we say?"

"He was in the bar when I got there, and as I've already told you I never laid eyes on him before."

"Even though you are there frequently, and he is a regular?"

As this is more than even *he's* willing to put up with he makes to get out, but, turning around, Guzman says, "Both the *capitan* and I have only your best interests at heart, and having come into possession of certain information regarding this individual he intends looking more closely into his history."

"What exactly has he supposed to have done?"

"Let's just say our own Spanish womenfolk have little to fear from what he keeps in his trousers. Remember what we did with that *maricon* Lorca in Granada? Put a round up his arse, then dumped him in a ditch along with some of those other nancy boy commie pals of his. But filth like that are like weeds that sprout in the dark, and even if a foreign passport stands in our way we still must keep a close eye on what they're up to while in our country."

He gives a laugh.

"Not that anyone would ever suspect a *macho hombre* such as yourself of being inclined that way, we know only too well where your affections lie. So go home to your bachelor bed where someone more accommodating than you might imagine could soon be joining you there."

Walking away, still smarting over what he'd just heard, instead of his usual route back to the apartment he realises he's heading towards the beach, which was where he'd first encountered that mysterious "someone" Guzman had just mentioned. Seeing him then, she'd quickened her pace, and not wishing to cause alarm he should have left it at that instead of addressing her with a *"buenas noches, senora,"* and turning, she stared directly, almost fiercely at him with no trace of subservience in that look.

After she disappeared into the gathering darkness he'd continued staring after her, like someone half, even a quarter his years mooning over the unattainable at some village dance in some parochial hall somewhere.

Yet he couldn't dismiss her from his head, and a week later when he saw her again he told himself some sort of inevitability must be at work here. Inside the hotel the encounter took place and he was with Guzman who was boasting of his relations with the manager.

"We regularly play cards in his office along with the *capitan,* and it wouldn't do you any harm to join us in a hand there yourself. But that will keep for later. Right now, allow me to give you the guided tour."

Led outside he'd been shown the pool area with its ranks of precisely arranged sun-loungers supporting all those slowly browning bodies, Guzman strutting, eager to impress, for despite all of that arrogance Furlong could see he was in awe of anyone born to more money than himself.

Next he was taken indoors to admire the vast dining-room set for dinner, a row of waiters standing to attention, and then they took the lift, and when they reached the top floor, he was ushered out on to a long thickly carpeted corridor.

"I want you to see the presidential suite where the Caudillo himself will take up residence when he comes to stay," said

Guzman, going to a telephone on the wall, while an already bored Furlong drifted on ahead peering at the cardboard signs on the door handles in four languages.

When he was as far as the very last bedroom he heard the lift doors open, and turning, expecting to see one of Don Gustavo's flunkies, he saw it was the woman from the *playa*, but dressed in an hotel uniform and carrying a bunch of keys in her hand.

"Open this door for the Irish senor and myself," commanded Guzman, standing outside room 503 where the great man himself would lay his famous bald head on his long promised trip south, and, approaching, the woman shot a glance at Furlong from those fierce dark eyes of hers just as she'd done on the beach that evening.

Turning the key in the lock, she stood aside to allow them to enter, Guzman ordering her to draw the heavy curtains for the interior was as dark and airless as a tomb. However, she still hung back in the doorway, so Guzman crossed to a switch, and the room, more like a palatial suite than any hotel room, was instantly lit by twin lamps on either side of the enormous canopied bed, Furlong visualising that small figure lying at its heart like a bald baby in an over-sized cot.

"Well, what is it? Afraid he might be watching you?" Guzman sneered, there being several Franco portraits about the walls.

"Don Gustavo is the only person with permission to enter here. He says nothing must be disturbed."

Hearing her voice for the first time was not what he imagined it would be, softer, refined, even, in some way, unlike the grating Andalusian accents he was used to.

Turning to him, Guzman murmured, "This republican bitch still hasn't learned humility, her manners, either."

He was speaking in English but from the look on her face Furlong felt she understood, so he said, "She's only following orders."

"If I had my say it would've been a shaved head and a *paseo* through the streets along with all the rest of her *rojo* sisters."

Then in a complete turn-around, reverting to Spanish, addressing her, he said, "I was glad, Adriana, to hear you'd found employment here. In our own way we must all learn to put the past behind us, and so I'm pleased to see you so protective of the Caudillo's privacy even if he can't be here in person to appreciate it."

Walking off down the corridor along with Guzman to take the lifts once more, it's all he can do to keep from looking over his shoulder, knowing now as he does that the person still standing back there is someone he must meet with again if only to satisfy this strange, unsettling longing which has taken such a hold on him.

ADRIANA

Throughout the first weeks of July the *terral* is blowing, its dry, scorching breath confining the hotel guests to their rooms, so overseeing the cleaning and changing of the linen is a daily struggle before presenting her written record at the end of her shift to Don Gustavo. On the Monday, however, it became clear he'd more pressing concerns than insuring the clients had fresh sheets, soap or sufficient towels for their needs.

Word had leaked out that someone important might be coming to the Miramar, even speculation that Francisco Franco Bahamonde himself was to honour them with a surprise visit.

Earlier she and Carlotta had been in her domain below drinking their first *café nero* of the day and Carlotta was saying, "I've never cooked for anyone so grand before. They say he has a delicate constitution and can only tolerate consomme, while here we fry everything, not like in Galicia."

Where he's been harder on his own people up there than

anywhere else, floated dangerously into her head, while wondering what Diego would say if she told him Frank the Frog might be coming through the doors of her hotel with that usual bunch of hard-faced lackeys at his back.

"Do you think we'll get up close to him?"

And so again there comes the urge to tell her friend it wasn't the Redeemer Himself descending in an aeroplane from Madrid but the same *puta madre* responsible for her husband hiding himself away in the dark these twenty-odd long years. Suddenly, despite the heat, she feels herself grow cold as even *thinking* such things can be dangerous.

"Still, if he does decide to stay be sure to tell us of his personal requirements."

"Personal requirements?"

"Yes, you know, one pillow or two, silk sheets instead of cotton, an eiderdown, that kind of thing."

"He's bound to have his own people taking care of such matters."

However, she appeared disappointed Adriana might not get to find out the brand of the great man's cologne, soap, tooth powder, moustache pomade.

Then Carlotta said something unexpected.

"My Manolo, God rest him, would turn in his grave to learn I'd ever made soup for the General."

Even though they were alone together in that great white-tiled basement, the cook's voice had dropped to a near whisper, and Adriana felt her own chest tighten, for in all the time they'd known one another Carlotta had never given the slightest hint their husbands might have shared similar views, even if one was dead, and the other was not.

Still, as though realising she might have left herself vulnerable, Carlotta rose, and going to her pots and pans began lifting their lids and sniffing and stirring the contents, so Adriana knew their morning coffee and gossip time had come to an end.

Some while later, walking along a hushed upper corridor, she found herself checking the shoes left outside each door to be cleaned, for Teo the boot boy still hadn't collected them, or perhaps he had.

Taking note of every size and style, she could practically tell the owner's nationality from what she'd seen in the rooms themselves. Here, the stout German's hiking boots waxed to a permanent shine, there, the businessman from Cordoba's crocodile leather pumps, next door, the English gentleman's brogues. Once a pair of jackboots complete with spurs had given her a nasty turn, made worse on seeing the military uniform laid out on the bed. Whoever it was, however, he'd only stayed the one night.

Having completed her slow, steady patrol, something made her take to the stairs instead of the lift down one flight, only realising on emerging it was the *Americano's* floor.

Ever since that night when she'd half-carried him along this identical stretch of corridor, in a kind of dread she'd been waiting for him to remember. Not that she'd any desire for recognition or reward, for it had been a foolish act on her part which might yet return to punish her.

Yet here she was revisiting the scene of the crime, as it were, and gazing down the long stretch of corridor she saw that something was amiss. All the shoes were in disarray as if someone had gone along kicking them left and right, and so it came to her who the culprit had to be, drunkenly scattering other peoples' property, with one of his own loafers lying adrift three doors further along.

And still not knowing why she persisted in having this stranger's welfare at heart, taking it up, she laid it outside room 404 where it belonged, and began returning all the other shoes to their rightful places for their owners to retrieve when they eventually stirred.

Below in the basement the doors of the washers and driers there already lay open for the first loads of the day. Going along the line she peered into each one to make sure nothing was left inside, for once a rogue red sock had nearly caused disaster before bleach saved the day, and she still remembered the panic, five people staring in horror at the pink sheets before she took control. One of the younger washerwomen started wailing and crying.

"Stop that, Ampora, do you hear me? Or do you want those *gringos* upstairs thinking we're all a bunch of hopeless cases?" and it was like the old days all over again when she rallied the women in the pueblo, persuading them to march to the town hall with the men. That was another time when flags and ribbons the same colour as the sock flew from every home, every hen-coop, every bicycle, even the very donkeys sported banners. Now the only shade of *rojo* to be seen was on some foreigner's hose left lying in the drum of a washing machine.

After she spoke, there was silence, then one of the other women addressed the others.

"Listen and pay heed to Adriana, for she's one of us and we

49

can trust her not to go telling tales to those who would break our bones."

At the time it was a speech almost as surprising as Carlotta's earlier, and for a moment she felt perhaps some tiny flame of revolt still flickered of the kind Diego believed would one day flare up again, listening to his radio, or reading the newspapers she brought him. After they'd finished with them the guests would leave them in their rooms, and even if he couldn't understand all the words he would pore over them with a dictionary at his side hoping to sift some unbiased reporting from their pages.

Once, leaving the hotel, one of them fell out of her bag, and picking it up, Don Gustavo said, "What are you doing with this lying foreign rubbish when you can have my own *Arriba* or *ABC* for the asking?" and she'd fed him a story about taking it home to line some cupboard drawers there which seemed to satisfy him.

Looking back on both these episodes, she realised she might have left herself open to something which could come back to harm her, and later that morning her fears were realised.

At eight-thirty the first police cars started drawing up outside, so the rumours about an important visitor arriving seemed to be correct after all, and some little while later when she was on the upper floors she encountered that local Guardia Civil captain, Delgado coming out of the lift accompanied by some of his men.

She'd been in one of the vacated rooms with Juanita who was new and still needed supervision. Making beds, dusting and cleaning came naturally to her, but as she'd never seen a bathtub, even a wash-basin before, she was nervous, while as for that other shameless foreign object alongside the lavatory she was especially wary of it after Adriana explained its purpose. Crossing herself before flushing it, she peered into its china bowl as though visualising what the couple in the room might have been up to prior to making use of it.

Seeing Adriana with the house keys and the cleaning roster in her hand, the police captain ordered her, "Let me have a look at that," meaning the book with the names of the guests occupying each room.

Taking it from her, he flicked through it, finally running a finger down one page.

"How many more floors require your attention?"

"Only the remaining top two."

"Well, leave them just as they are and make sure no-one has access to *numero cinco*. Do I make myself clear?"

"Si, senor *capitan*."

Handing back the record book, he stared at her.

"Your name?"

She tells him, and once more he fixes her with that unwavering policeman's stare, almost as regulation as the belted uniform and *pistola* he carries.

"Do I know you? Have we met before?"

"No, senor."

Then he says, "Room 404. Are you familiar with the person occupying that room?"

Realising it's the *Americano,* she cautions herself to be extra careful.

"Tell me does the gentleman there ever have company?"

"Company, senor?"

51

Again that same look drilling her.

"Are you aware of traces of anyone else sharing it, I mean. In the bed, for instance? Certain personal items in the bathroom?"

"Even if there were, it's none of my business, senor, nor the chamber-maids', either."

Hearing this, he laughs, which should have been a relief, but isn't, for the eyes remain hard, black as coal, like the moustache, yet another police trademark.

Before turning away, he salutes, accompanied by a click of the heels.

"Don't let me detain you from your duties, senora. And I trust I can still count on your vigilance regarding those who might not share the same respect for the Caudillo and the *patria* as the rest of us do."

After he'd gone, taking the lift at the end of the corridor, she feels herself quake, for that menace still lingers.

Below in the vestibule itself she's met by a scene of milling confusion, a white-faced Don Gustavo flapping his pale little hands, calling out, *"Todo! Todo!"* for everyone to assemble by the front desk.

Some of the hotel staff already have emerged, brushing down their overalls, wiping their palms along the seams of their trousers like children preparing for a surprise school inspection. Even the breakfast waiters have deserted their stations, and at the back she can see Carlotta and her helpers in their kitchen whites and aprons.

Taking her place on the fringes of the crowd, she stands waiting for Don Gustavo to address them all, even feeling a quickening of anticipation herself at finally getting to see their visitor. Then behind her the lift doors slide open and the police captain steps out to stand alongside the manager who announces, "In recognition of all our efforts in promoting and celebrating the appeal and charms of this most beautiful region of our beloved Espana, Don Antonio Ramirez, Minister for the Interior with Special Responsibility for Tourism, will be arriving shortly as an honoured guest of the Miramar."

Here he paused, and putting his glasses on, produced a piece of paper, preparing to read from it. But before he's able to speak, raising a hand in the air, the police captain delivers a statement of his own.

"Throughout the duration of the Minister's stay here, I, Captain Enrique Delgado, will be in charge of his personal security, and so let me caution you that any careless talk or gossip going beyond these four walls will be severely dealt with."

Don Gustavo murmurs something to him, and they hear the policeman reply, "Very well, let us begin with a preliminary inspection of the kitchens."

Carlotta's standing not far away so Adriana is able to gauge her reaction, seeing her move surprisingly quickly for such a large woman towards the service stairs as though even pots and pans might have the power to convict, and after Don Gustavo and the captain have taken the lift people start glancing nervously around them, whispering among themselves.

At this point the telephone on the front desk rings, all eyes turning in its drection, one of the new, younger waiters, Pepe, looking as though he might make a move towards it himself, before freezing under the weight of the crowd's silent disapproval, and so it goes on trilling until whoever's on the other end hangs up.

Starting to wonder how Carlotta might be getting on with the captain's "inspection", she feels a hand on her arm, Concepta, one of the upstairs maids, sidling up to her.

"Dona Adriana," she whispers, "I left my bag with my papers in it in one of the rooms."

"And was there anything else inside?"

Her face goes pale.

"Some rouge and lip paint the lady in three-o-five gave me."

"Don't worry, Don Gustavo only ever wears Spanish Puig himself."

For a moment the sturdy peasant woman stares at her, then a grin creases her dark face.

"The German senora also gave me a pair of her *bragas*, her silk knickers."

"In your size?"

"Si, *muy, muy grande*."

It's a rare moment of shared humour between the two of them, supervisor and cleaning maid, reverting to how it once was before the country's "long night of stone" set in.

It's close to eleven-thirty now, yet there's still no sign of Don Gustavo, Captain Delgado, neither, and the young waiter who looked poised to go to the phone earlier is tapping his feet and humming loudly to himself for not everyone's cowed by authority.

Just then the telephone rings for a second time, again no one daring to answer it, not even Pepe, and so it goes on and on, until finally someone calls out, "Adriana! Adriana! Dona

Adriana!" and unable to ignore the demand she crosses the expanse of marble floor, praying the thing will fall silent before she gets to it.

Putting the receiver to her ear, she hears an official-sounding voice on the other end informing her that Don Ramirez and his party have landed at Malaga airport and are now on their way to the hotel.

"Have all the Minister's personal requirements been taken care of?"

"Si, senor."

"His official security detail standing by?"

"Si, senor."

"As this is his first official visit the utmost discretion and confidentiality must be observed at all times. Do I make myself clear?"

"Si, senor."

"Very well, be ready to expect us shortly."

However, before she's able to take all this in there's a further ring, not from the telephone still in her hand, but over at the lifts, everyone turning expecting to see Don Gustavo and the police captain step out. But someone else appears, the one some in the hotel have already nicknamed *el medio sordo*, the half-deaf one, and for an instant he looks confused as though decidng to travel back up again to that permanently darkened room of his on the fourth floor.

Eager to attract his attention, Pepe calls out, "Senor Johnnie! Senor Johnnie!" but instead the Americano walks towards another of the young *camareros* standing there, the one in charge of the Hollywood Room.

For Pepe it's a serious humiliation, and Jorge himself looks embarrassed, framed in the doorway of his bar, empty of patrons at this hour, save, of course, for someone in urgent need of a drink. Knowing what's on this foreigner's mind, suddenly Adriana feels this unexpected private ache for him, until someone in the crowd pipes up, "Gone a *poco* bit hard of hearing yourself, Jorge, have you?" a ripple of laughter breaking out, the Americano grinning, too.

The mood having now lightened, people start moving about, nodding, smiling at one another, until the lift lights flash back on again, Don Gustavo stepping out looking flustered unlike the policeman whose expression seems even more frozen, making her wonder if Carlotta and her kitchens have been found wanting in some way.

Still, it's not her fat friend with a cause to be worried, but Adriana herself, Pepe blurting out, "Don Gustavo, Don Gustavo, while you were away a call came through on your telephone and Adriana answered it," and just when there seemed no possible way out for her, a car, this great gleaming limousine, the national colours flying from its prow, glided into sight outside.

The Minister when he climbs out is not as she expects, not short, plump and bald with a paunch like his master, but tall with a hawkish profile and a fine head of silvery grey hair.

He's talking now with one of his aides, a younger man in a dark suit who's pointing up at the exterior of the building as though briefing him on its history, until finally the glass entrance doors are thrown open and Don Ramirez strides inside to stand for a moment gazing up at the famous mural with its scenes of Andalusian peasant life and happy, smiling fishing folk.

From his gestures the one who has the ear of the Minister seems suggesting the visitors should make their way to the bar, but Don Gustavo and the police captain instead are indicating the dining-room where the tables are already laid, Adriana wondering if Carlotta has been informed of this development.

However, surely she must have been, and seeing her move quickly towards the back stairs, still avoiding her glance, she feels a pang of betrayal, and as the day progresses the sensation hardens, even the cleaning women chattering among themselves about topics which seem to have been kept from her.

Locking herself in one of the vacated rooms, she sits on the bed, until hearing a noise in the corridor, noises, for the sound is a burst of laughter coming from the maids, she rises, automatically smoothing the coverlet as though she's never been here.

Juanita, the one she'd been joking with earlier, is outside, so she asks her, "What's happening?"

"They're going to take a photograph of us all with the Minister."

Then, with a grin, she says, "Do you want to borrow some of the foreign lady's lip paint?" before walking off, patting her hair as though already primping herself for the camera.

After she's gone, brazenly taking the lift instead of the stairs, Adriana stands there as though she's the last one left on these upper floors.

At the end of the corridor, above the table there with its jug of freshly cut lilies, a mirror's been placed, so female guests can catch a final appraising glance at themselves before going downstairs. Catching a glimpse of her own reflection there, this pale, unsmiling village woman, relic of another time and place, it strikes her she may have become frozen in time like Diego himself, and perhaps others can see it as well.

In the foyer below, as Juanita had said, it seems as though nearly everyone employed in the place apart from herself is now gathered there, with a photographer darting about holding a viewfinder to one eye.

Eventually, while they watch, one of the waiters, the one they call the *mayordomo*, throws opens the doors of the dining-room, and looking suitably refreshed the official party appears to take up their positions in front of the reception desk for a photograph for the Malaga papers.

After more of the same Don Gustavo seems now to be pleading for a group shot of the Miramar's assembled staff, arranging people in order of their ranking, and so Adriana waits to be ushered forward herself.

But instead he motions her to remain with the cleaning women, even the kitchen porters and gardeners, who look sideways at her wondering what she's done to merit such an humiliation, that earlier business with the telephone possibly the reason.

After the camera flashes, everyone smiling as though at a wedding, the Minister and his little group make their way towards the lifts and people start drifting off to their respective duties, some of the guests appearing looking confused as though they've overslept, stupefied by the motion of all those overhead fans.

The rest of the day, a general air of restiveness prevails, no one quite able to give themselves over to the tasks they normally perform. In one of the rooms she comes upon an unflushed toilet and finds herself yelling at the maid responsible that people no longer need relieve themselves on the sierra like animals.

When her shift finishes, taking her record book, she goes down as usual for Don Gustavo to check its tally. Coming out of the lifts, however, she sees the entire foyer's now crowded with strangers all decked out as though for some function, the women in their most expensive evening gowns.

From where she's standing, back against the chill metal of the lift doors, she can see Don Gustavo himself in a sleek dark evening suit, with some people she recognises, Delgado and Guzman the Crab with two others she's no wish to meet with again, either at night on the *playa* or here in the hotel, the Americano and that ruddy-faced *irlandes* with the limp. He and the singer have glasses in their hands and are laughing together.

She could take the service stairs, of course, but she still has the cleaning roster for Don Gustavo, so she edges her way forward intending to leave it on the reception desk and so avoid the manager who's clearly more concerned with his guests than bother about such trifling matters as checking on towels, sheets or toilet paper.

When she's only a short distance away, one of the guests, a blonde woman, clearly taking her for one of the serving staff, clutches her arm, ordering her, "Fetch me another glass of champagne," and so she stares at her as though the woman had spoken in a foreign tongue.

"And while you're at it one of those little canape things, an *empanadilla*," a word she *is* familiar with.

"Well, don't just stand there like a *pueblovina*."

But this blonde-haired bitch, with the bare shoulders of a *puta*, will just have to get someone else to serve her, and moving on she reaches the desk unnoticed, leaving her book there, planning on sidling back into the crowd and taking the back stairs to the kitchens and off into the night. Except, feeling another tug on her sleeve, it's Don Gustavo himself, hissing in her ear, "Can't you see this is an official function for the Minister. It's not appropriate for someone like yourself to be here at this time."

Having penned her into an alcove, his tone's now one of hurt bewilderment.

"How could you disappoint me in this way after me giving you the gift of my generosity as I did? God knows, I'm some-one who believes the past is dead and buried, but there are others with long memories, not so forgiving. It's *them* I have to accommodate for the good reputation of the Miramar, can't you see that?"

But, oh, she can, she can, after possibly the longest speech ever to come from this man in front of her.

"You must go now, for the Minister will be down any second. You and I will discuss this further in the morning as well as your future employment here. Changes are in the air, some of which may affect not just you, but every one of us here at the Miramar."

Making her way to the *cocinas* below, her new invisibility holds good, all those toiling there oblivious to her presence, a sweating, purple-faced Carlotta hauling trays from the ovens, and so she glides through, an anonymous ghost in her outdoor clothes in a sea of kitchen whites.

JOHNNIE

This time around the bedside phone didn't ring with his usual wake-up call but he didn't need a reminder anyway, feeling more rested than he remembers for a long time, and lying there a tune worms its way into his head and him recalling how he and his sister Elma practically wore it out on their old Victrola. "Smoke Dreams", the Jo Stafford version.

Even though they do have piped music in the Hollywood Room it's only syrupy string arrangements and Mario Lanza vocals and he's asked Jorge to change the track which is like persuading him to take down one of the photographs off the wall, preferably Frankie's, that frozen grin of his up there reminding him of how that skinny Wop sonofabitch tried to sabotage his career when Ava made a play for him. Sinatra's never forgiven him for it, even though Ava was the one who made the move, not him.

Still, this is not the time or place to get hung up over The

Voice when out there this big *feria* shindig's about to kick off that Minister of Tourism and Interior guy sounded so upbeat about. Having been introduced to him the night of the reception, Senor Ray was the very essence of tact and diplomacy even when Senor Ramirez professed his deep admiration for Senator McCarthy and his campaign to root out those commies back home along with Jews, blacks and homos.

A waiter just then was passing with drinks and scooping a glass of *cava* from the tray Johnnie downed it in one while Don Gustavo hovered nearby clearly worried some sort of international incident might not be far off. But he had no reason for alarm, Senor Ray responding with, "You must forgive a humble entertainer who knows very little about politics."

"Even so, you could help in promoting a deeper understanding between our two nations, even if, as I'm given to understand, your time here with us is limited."

Relishing the barely concealed look of nervousness on Don Gustavo's face, Johnnie told him, "You never know, I might just stick around a little longer than originally planned."

And why not, he's thinking now, for when was the last time he'd had a proper break? He can't remember, and drinking oneself into a nightly stupor doesn't really count, and so he looks at the telephone, not to answer it, but make the call himself, telling Bernie to shift some dates around ... Then again, perhaps later. Or, as they say out here, *manana*.

Having showered, shaved, he's agreeably surprised at how steady his hand is, already looking forward to his first proper daylight foray outside the hotel, save for that episode with the cop on the beach that time and the gypos who'd rolled him there, presumably now staring at some scribbled-on cell wall somewhere.

The prospect of mingling with the locals in festive mood has him feeling pumped up, and going to the closet he picks out something appropriate, jeans and a navy blue polo shirt, dark glasses supplying the required finishing touch of anonymity. Until, standing there hand on the door-knob, he remembers the hearing-aid.

Early on he'd learned to lip-read, so he's weighing up whether to leave it behind or not, as being with a bunch of strangers mouthing in another tongue renders it pretty superfluous anyway. However, mind made up, stepping out into the corridor, hopefully just like any other tourist in a pair of Polaroids, he heads downstairs, and disguise working well in reception, the clerk behind the desk there barely gives him a passing glance.

Outside the hotel's heavy glass doors the temperature arrives as a shock, the hairs on his arms prickling, sweat pooling in the small of his back, and standing on the front steps he's debating whether the dim coolness of the bar might not be a better alternative after all. Still, no turning back, he tells himself, making for the shady side of the street leading to where most of the action seems to be taking place.

Even without the hearing-aid he can sense a heavy throbbing in the air that can only come from drums, overlaid by a screech of brass, this mass of people all now moving in the same direction as himself, grandmothers and women carrying babies, serious-faced men in white shirts, entire families, and in the midst of this peasant stream a small posse of horses and riders, heads held patricianly high as they trot past.

Arriving at what seems the central meeting point, there's a strong smell of grilling fish in the air, people clutching beer bottles, someone pressing a full one into his hand, this grinning young kid who might be a waiter on his day off, and for an instant he stands there feeling isolated and out of things among all these strangers intent on having themselves a good time.

Some way off to his right lies the usual flotilla of beached fishing-boats now drawn up on the sand. They look as if they've had a fresh coat of paint, several with that Moorish blue eye on the prow to ward off bad luck, and making his way to the water's edge he spots this tiny encampment of young hippies sprawled on the sand with their guitars and bongo drums. They're smoking pot, he can smell it, and he's about to take his chances among the locals again, when one of them, this skinny bearded Jesus freak in an Afghan coat despite the heat, hails him before he's time to retreat.

"Hey, come and hang out, man. Where are you from?"

Even without his ear-piece, he can tell he's American, and not having heard the accent since he's been here he has this sudden twinge of home sickness. One of the girls in the party now extending an invitation of her own.

"Yeah, come and join us. You here for the Virgin?"

Back to reading lips again, he's confused, for did she actually say *virgin*? Or was it in the plural, clearly having jettisoned her own virtue some way back.

A leggy blonde with long straight hair falling to her waist, and wearing denim cut-offs and cowboy boots, she's clearly giving him the come-on. Yet what makes it even more flattering is that none of these kids have the foggiest idea who he is, and so he joins them, even taking a drag on the joint offered directly from the blonde's lips.

Entering into the spirit of it, he squats there, silently translating what's being said. It turns out they've been drifting along the coast towards Tarifa where they've heard the surf is as good as at Big Sur, the Atlantic breakers the size of a two-storey house. Right now they've no boards, but aim to get some when they reach their destination.

"Providence provides, brother," says the one who hailed him first, and the others nod in agreement before inhaling some of that grade A weed with plenty more where that comes from. Despite all their hippy talk he can tell they've enough to survive on here where the peseta's weak and the dollar's climbing in value daily. These are spoilt rich kids rebelling against the American way of life, another generation and world away from his own background there.

One even has a tee-shirt with Eat The Rich across the front, while another reads, Property Is Theft, making him wonder what they really think of him in his Sachs labels, that's if they *think* at all, the mood being one of deep down, unconditional love, man, the blonde's hand now resting on his thigh.

"What's your name, man? Whaddya they call you?" someone unexpectedly enquires, as this far no introductions have been forthcoming as though unnecessary, un-cool, even.

"Johnnie," he tells him, this serious kid with a full Afro, unlike the other males in the company, "Johnnie," for a brief moment teetering on the brink of throwing in a surname, and the kid, most definitely a touch of color there, says, "I'm Leon," reaching out a fist, and they bump knuckles together.

Time drifts, only the lapping of the waves on the shingle

65

invading their consciousness, the noise from the crowds having receded as though they're quarantined in their own private little universe. No longer hunkered, but lying outstretched on the sand, he's studying this small, perfectly motionless cirrus formation pinned against the blue above, until, eyes closed, he starts humming to himself, finally seguing into the lyrics of something he's performed a hundred times or more, but never to a bunch of hopped-up, stoned love children on a beach before, that first big number one of his, "The Little White Cloud That Cried", and they all lie listening to it there in doped silence.

"Wow, that's really beautiful, man. What is it? I never heard it before," murmurs the one in the Afghan coat, and sliding her hand a fraction closer to his crotch, the girl lazily concurs.

"Pure poetry. Way out."

Then Leon says, "This aunt of mine used to have this bunch of old records she would always play. Some guy, can't remember his name?"

"Ray," he tells him, "Johnnie Ray."

Yet still the dime doesn't drop, the blonde commenting, "Same name as yours, eh? Johnnie, I mean. Kinda weird, don't you think?"

After that no one says anything, allowing their thoughts to drift like that little streak of lint unravelling high above until nothing's left of it on that bare canvas up there slowly darkening to the same shade of blue as the shirt he's wearing.

Still, he must have dozed off, for when next he looks up the sky's full of swifts wheeling and dive-bombing so spectacularly he's happily content to just stay here for as long as the show lasts.

"You ready to move on, man?" says Afghan Coat, breaking in. " You don't wanna miss it when they carry the Virgin into the sea."

Still feeling woozy he stares up at him until Leon explains about the procession leaving the church once a year and the statue being brought out and launched on the water to bless the fishing-boats.

Reaching down, the Blonde hoists him up to her own level.

"Come on, it'll be cool, you'll see."

"Yeah, let's go, man, the night is young."

"And we are beautiful!" somebody else calls out, and everyone laughs, although actually it does seem that way.

Afghan Coat, taking the lead, they wind their unsteady way up the beach towards the seafront where it looks like the crowds are already assembling before heading for the church one street back. Even with *his* crummy hearing he can make out the clamour of bells, high pitched, clanging, Arabic-sounding, unlike the ones back home, not that he's any kind of a church-going authority, not since he played the organ and sang in his local Lutheran where it all began for him.

Inside a matter of minutes he and his little band of new-found *amigos* are swallowed up by the faithful inching forward in this near solid mass, the heat, an overpowering smell of stale sweat, scent and cologne making his head swim.

The girl, he still hasn't caught her name, is holding on tight to him.

"Don't lose me, you promise? Promise?"

Mouthing back, he tells her, "I'm right here. I'm not going anywhere," jammed in tight as they all are, until he sees Afghan Coat up ahead with his hand in the air as though drawing their attention to the night sky, starless and almost ink-black by now. But instead he's pointing towards the balconies on either side of the street and people hanging out there looking down, and next instant he seems to be directing them to this doorway like the entrance to a bar, leaving them wondering whether to tag after him or not.

However, as Blondie's tugging hard on his arm, the decision already looks made for him, and following after her, the interior beyond, dark and empty for some reason, is like this oasis of calm where refreshments are on hand even if there's no one's there to serve them. And seeing that hallowed trio, San Miguel, Cruz Campo, Estrella, lined up in front of him, despite having vowed to take things slow, he decides he badly needs a drink after all.

"Where's he got to? Where the fuck is he?" young Leon complains, until somebody jerks a thumb at the ceiling, grinning, as though he's in on it, and Blondie tells him not to be an asshole, and next minute they're all bitching away like a bunch of kids at summer camp, and so *he* suggests, "Okay, so why don't we just check it out upstairs?" even though right then he'd kill for a cold beer.

"Johnnie's right," says Leon. "We should listen to him instead of just horsin' around and wasting time."

Suddenly they're all looking at him and so he points towards a door and this narrow flight of stairs there, and getting himself an eyeful of that tight young denim-clad butt directly ahead of him, he follows it on and up. Reaching the top, however, instantly it becomes apparent this has been one seriously bad move on their part gate-crashing somebody's private family gathering with all these locals glaring at this bunch of young *vagabundo* types now jostling in the doorway.

One of them, this up-market looking dude in a white suit with a flower in its button hole, growls something in Spanish sounding threatening, reinforced by the grim look on his face, Afghan Coat reacting swiftly, "Forgive the intrusion, senor, but Paco invited us to come and join you to watch the procession up here with you," realising, as he must have done, everyone present there had to know someone with that name.

"Paco? From the bar? *Comprende?*"

Standing there in his beat-up old sheepskin coat reeking of weed, he's displaying all the cheek of the born con artist.

Over on the other side of the room, propped up in a high-backed chair on the veranda overlooking the street, is this old crone, who without turning her head spits out something, even Johnnie detecting the venom there.

Right then, however, everything changes, for the guy in the expensive suit is staring, not at Afghan Coat, but at *him* hanging back in the doorway already poised to make a getaway.

"Senor? Senor Ray, is it really *you?*" he says, coming forward, hand outstretched, a smile on his handsome features.

"What an honour to have you here in my grandmother's house," he announces. Then, after the barest hesitation, "And, naturally, your young friends, also," all of whom are staring now in *his* direction for the guy's English is pretty good so that even they've got the message, especially Afghan Coat, chipping in with, "As Senor Ray expressed a wish to see your famous ceremony we asked him to come along as well."

It turns out their host was present at the reception for the Tourism minister the other night, and having now manoeuvred him into a corner, he enquires, "These charming young *compadres* of yours, they, too, are American?"

He tells him they met only recently and by chance, which is true, and by another coincidence, are fans of his music, which isn't, and the factory owner, for that's what he is, says, "My good friend Captain Delgado, who I understand you've met, tells me he's also something of an *admirador*. But then I suppose no matter where you travel your popularity attracts all kinds of attention from those flattered at being seen in your company."

Getting the distinct impression he's being schmoozed now, he's relieved when old granny on the balcony suddenly becomes animated, the children being pushed forward for a better view of what's taking place in the street below.

"Come, sit here, senor," White Suit commands, making room for him beside his wizened relative. "They're about to carry our famous statue out from the church," crossing himself, as indeed they all are now, even Afghan Coat brushing his chest in a one-fingered variation of his own.

Perched, knees pressed against the bars of the balcony, he lets his gaze travel out over the bared heads of the faithful below, all now turned towards the open doors of the church. There's silence. Then, when the priest appears on the steps, the storm breaks, this great exhalation of pent up adulation pouring forth accompanied by the bells cracking open the night sky, and unexpectedly, he feels a weird kind of buzz himself, what's happening next unfolding like some lavish Hollywood spectacular, as down the steps comes this slow-stepping procession of barefoot men and boys in sailor suits holding the Virgin aloft, swaying on her pedestal, cradling the baby Jesus.

"Wow, like somethin' out of a movie," breathes Blondie.

"Bride of Frankenstein", you mean?" quips Afghan Coat, and despite not knowing the language the old lady glares at him, so Johnnie throws in a *dominus vobiscum*, only scrap of Latin he knows, and she pats him on the knee.

Outside the church there appears to be some kind of a hiccup in the proceedings, a bunch of guys in more senior uniforms waving their arms about while the bearers stand patiently by holding their burden high.

Finally there's movement, and the band which has been standing easy all this time comes out with this ear-splitting overture, the crowd contributing a creepy Arabic sounding screech all their own sending shivers down the spine, and young Leon who's right behind him, murmurs, "Ain't this some kinda voodoo shit, or ain't it?"

Then, putting him on the spot, he says, "You're that singer we were talking about earlier, right?" So he nods, and the kid says, "Respect, man, respect", giving him a high-five.

Moments later, all those present seem to be getting ready to move to join the party below, the host telling him, "My *abuela* is much too frail for all of this excitement and so I must stay with her. But, *amigo*, you should go and enjoy the occasion with your young friends."

Parting company, they shake hands, traces of the other's cologne lingering on Johnnie's palm, until going down the stairs, detecting a much less innocent aroma, he realises Afghan Coat has lit up a fresh joint even before hitting the street.

Down below, the bar's still deserted, everyone having now gone on ahead, leaving him staring at the bottles lined temptingly up there in front of him. But the urgent need for another drink has gone, and even though there's nothing between him and all that craziness out there save a flimsy curtain of hanging plastic, he feels isolated inside his own world, the watch on his wrist telling him very nearly an entire day has flown by, most of it lost in a hazy blue blur like those long summer afternoons when he used to lie out in some cornfield staring up at an American sky instead of a Mediterranean one.

The tide of people in the street outside appears to have ebbed away by now, and following the sound of the music he heads in the direction of the sea. Standing in a doorway is a gaggle of senoritas in traditional costume, mascara-lined eyes, plum-red lips, tar-black hair, and as he walks past one of them calls out something, possibly filthy, for Spanish women as he's discovered can be nearly as foul-mouthed as their menfolk.

Even so, an expression, or rather, a word, rings a bell with him, *ciego*, blind, and realising it's the dark glasses, he takes them off, bowing, and they give him the bird, then a burst of clapping followed by a fusillade of foot-stamping.

Down along the water's edge where the beached fishing boats lie in rows on the sand, the Virgin's being readied for her annual dip in the ocean, her attendants, sailor pants rolled above the knee, preparing to wade out with her.

Staring sightlessly ahead, the bald infant Jesus in her arms, she floats off on her candle-lit raft of flowers, a tremendous shout instantly going up, followed by fireworks. Other craft too, lit up bow to stern with coloured lanterns, keep her company, this one big white motor yacht coming in real close,

72

and seeing it out there he feels certain he recognises some of those on board who had been at the Minister's reception at the Miramar.

On the vessel's deck, a small combo's playing, and knowing the tune, "Besame Mucho", hearing someone else, a stranger, on the vocals, suddenly he has the feeling that if something were to happen to him here in the midst of all these people nobody would ever know.

However, just then, feeling a hand on his arm and turning round, the irony of it strikes him for out of this entire gathering has now stepped the one person with any sort of inkling of who he is after all, and he asks him, "Where have all the others got to?"

But Leon just looks at him in this real odd way as if something's happened to him, and possibly not good.

"What is it? Is everything okay?"

Still no reaction, just this unfocussed stare, and so it comes to him he must be stoned, before finally the kid manages to get something out, yet still sounding off the wall.

"You know Sammy Davis Junior? Eartha Kitt?"

"Yeah, been on TV shows with them both."

"Nat King Cole? Nina Simone? Harry Belafonte?"

It's beginning to sound like some weird kind of *Ebony* Poll of the Month now, and maybe it *is* his imagination but the kid's skin does appear to have got darker as well, while out there the Virgen del Carmen still floats serenely along towed by one of the fishing-boats low in the water on account of the weight of people on board.

"Sonofabitch called me a nigger back there. One of them SS Gestapo types, the pigs in uniform."

"You're sure of that?"

"Same word, negro, right? You don't have to know the fucking language."

He longs to offer something reassuring but can't think of anything. Anyway, the kid's eyes say it all, having lost that earlier stoned glaze and now popping with rancour.

"Look, it's just the way they are. Don't let it get to you."

"Gotta swallow enough of that KKK shit back home to have to take it here!"

"Even so, don't do anything stupid, you hear?" he advises, the kid coming back with, "As opposed to kissing uniformed Spanish ass, you mean?"

Nevertheless, he makes one final appeal.

"Now listen, take a look around. Isn't this what you came all this way here for? The *real* Spain? Well?"

"All I see are a bunch of Nazi storm-troopers," the kid spits in reply, pointing to a trio of Guardia Civil lounging in a doorway scanning faces in the crowd.

"Look, I gotta go meet some people. But, hey, we're bound to run across one another later, right?" the lie sounding unconvincing even to himself, and the kid says, "Sure, yeah, yeah, whatever," the two of them giving each other high fives, and glancing back at the three cops Johnnie realises they're definitely checking them out now because of the gesture.

"Take it easy, right? Don't do anything foolish, you hear?"

"You, too, man, you, too. See you around."

After the kid's slouched off, he moves along the seafront himself to where the crush isn't so oppressive, the air coming off the water a lot cooler here, and after a time he stops in the shadow of one of the upturned fishing-boats, while out there the Virgen's still being towed along on her floral bed before being brought back to her cage in the church for yet another year.

High above an invisible Africa, the moon's come out, casting a silvery ribbon across the water. As he watches, the Main Attraction Herself comes gliding along it, as though following a path directly to where he's standing, aware of some weird connection between that same ghostly female figure out there and another encountered in a dream along this same stretch of beach.

Yet something tells him it might not have been a dream after all. Rolling out of bed that following morning, his bare foot had made contact with this tiny metal disc, same face engraved on it as the one now slowly, silently, heading towards him. Same little medal he takes from his pocket now, turning it over in his palm as though it might yet yield up some clue to its mysterious owner who may know a lot more about that lost night than he does.

EUGENE

Luis Casares Guzman, to afford him his full title, was some-one who made it his business to get to know everyone else's, something made quickly apparent when Furlong first arrived here on this stretch of the *costa*. His own family middle name, Kiely, however, he kept to himself when signing the lease for the apartment with Guzman acting as go-between.

After the contract was official and he moved in he hoped to keep him at arm's length, but soon discovered he was like the creepers covering the walls of the block itself, once a sucker took hold it became impossible to dislodge. Furlong's mistake being to invite him inside some weeks later when that roving gaze of his fastened on the photograph of him and his old comrades in the Fifteenth Bandera.

He'd intended putting it away along with all of those other souvenirs from that earlier time, his Irish discharge papers, a religious medal handed out by the Bishop of Galway when he and the lads in the photo sailed for this country on the SS Ondura in '36, a postcard of Caceres before it was bombed by the Reds, a missal retrieved from the church there, again blown to smithereens by the Republicans, although why he'd held on to *that* was a mystery, having given up going to Mass some considerable time ago.

But just as he'd let himself drift from his early youthful religion, he allowed himself to go along with Guzman's perception of him as this heroic veteran returning to the country he'd once fought for on the same side as himself. It made life easier, as well as accruing certain benefits for someone still carrying a physical memento in the form of a gammy leg, even though he alone knew the injury had been sustained, not in a trench at Badajoz, but Watford on the A1 labouring there ten years later. It was *his* secret, just like Guzman's boastful fiction regarding his own so-called military past.

"You and I, my Irish amigo, fought against the Bolsheviks and their godless creed, and while you're a resident here that sacrifice will never be forgotten."

After that first encounter with *El Jaiba* the two seemed destined to keep on meeting, and it occurred to Furlong it might give rise to some sort of joint nickname, the pair sharing something not quite right with one, or, in Guzman's case, both legs.

However, if he ever had to explain just why he'd ended up here he would have found it difficult to answer, even to himself. Twenty years earlier, along with a bunch of other young fellows just off a boat, still wearing tweed suits and carrying ashplants, he had sailed here inflamed by the cinema newsreels back home of churches being torched, altars destroyed, nuns raped, priests murdered.

That youthful rush of blood then now seemed like it had affected someone else, certainly not the person presently nesting in Las Golondrinas like the swallows under its eaves and giving the block its name, and where at dusk he would watch them dart back and forth to their young, their eerie cries eclipsing the low roar of the incoming breakers on the beach two streets away.

In the remote locality where he grew up the coast was a place rarely, if ever, visited, their family farm buried deep in the countryside. At least it seemed that way to him and his young brothers and one sister. One old illustrated book in particular, only proper volume in the house besides a prayer book and an agricultural catalogue, supplied all the dream material for imaginary jaunts to a shore almost as exotic as those in *A Traveller's Tales Of The Seven Seas* by someone by the name of Colonel Bertram Willoughby-Snell.

After that hellish three day crossing to El Ferrol with the other volunteers, dipping one's toe in blue-green water and smelling the ozone could never really recapture that same youthful appeal again, every mother's son on board convinced that if the Atlantic swell didn't finish them off, then seasickness and the falling about below decks would.

Following that short-lived "crusade" of theirs, nobody wanted anything to do with them after word got back home about General O'Duffy's drunken carrying on and their own poor record there, so when the old man died and the farm was sold enough was left of his share to get him to England away from all the begrudgers and hypocrites, never to return, not even for a burial, although, as it happened, it was a funeral that revived the connection, even if at a distance.

A year before, he'd had a letter from his sister Brigid. At Cissie Byrnes' funeral, she wrote, she'd run into an old friend of his, Jack Early, who'd been asking after him and so she'd passed on his address.

For a long time, unable to put it away in the suitcase along with those other reminders of the past, the letter lay on the chest of drawers, and every so often he'd take it up and re-read the words there.

Two months later, returning from his regular morning walk along the beach, he found the old senora in the apartment above waiting for him in a state of barely contained excitement. The senor had had a caller, she said, another foreign gentleman who was staying at the big new hotel on the playa where all the rich tourists took their holidays. Unable to bear the thought of a follow-up knock on his door Furlong decided to go to the Miramar and confront an unwelcome visitor from the past, one he thought safely consigned to an image in a photograph at the bottom of a suitcase.

It was now eleven thirty, the rest of the day stretching ahead before that first late afternoon drink of his, but when he got to the hotel he already had a fair notion where his visitor might be. Walking into the Hollywood Room he saw that Jorge wasn't on duty, but another waiter was in his place.

Save for the same bored looking server reading the day's *Sur*, the place was deserted, and just as he was about to turn and leave he spotted a half-empty glass on the bar along with an opened packet of cigarettes, recognising a brand not seen for a decade or more, and he was still staring at that cream and buff Sweet Afton twenty when its owner emerged from the *servicios* in baggy khaki shorts and a Hawaiian type shirt, and who, seeing him, cried out, "Gene, Gene Furlong, is it yourself at all? It's Jack, Jack Early, your oul' mucker!"

Then letting loose a laugh slicing through the dead mid-morning stillness of the place, he bellowed, "Here, what is it you're havin'? By the expression on your kisser, I'd say you could do with a bracer."

"Ah, it's still a bit early for me."

"Not for me, it is, despite the surname. Come on, Eduardo, give this oul' amigo of mine the same as myself," Furlong watching the bottle of John Jameson, *his* bottle, being brought down from the top shelf.

Reluctant as he was to break a well established habit, the truth was he badly needed something to get him through this encounter.

"Good health and *slainte* to old comrades the last time you and me wore the khaki. Recall, do you, them First World War uniforms they kitted us out with? German trousers that'd fit Finn McCool and us getting thinner by the day."

Desperate to steer the conversation away from the one topic he was anxious to avoid, Furlong asked, "So what have you been up to yourself since?"

"Sure, ach, now I couldn't settle. Not after the way they treated the General, and him only stickin' up for what was right while that crowd back home let *us* do their dirty work for them. Never the same, he was, after the Brigade was disbanded. Broke his heart, it did."

Gesturing for a refill, he went on, "Heard tell *you* went to England. Done well for yourself, too."

"Ah, people say more than their prayers back home."

Early laughed.

"No harm in lettin' others blow your trumpet for you. Me, I took off to the States for a spell, land of opportunity and all that."

His accent had briefly taken on a trans-Atlantic twang, Furlong having come across a number of "returned Yanks" in his time, all with the same urge to talk big and impress the natives. But before any of that came about, fixing him with a sly look, Early asked, "So what's it like bein' the gentleman of leisure out here? And why this place?"

"Sort of ended up where the land meets the sea, you might say."

"Aye, the right pair of rollin' stones you and me turned out." He laughed.

"More like the proverbial bad penny in my own particular case. Tell me, will you ever forget the time..?"

While the foreign sun blazed outside, in the cool dimness of the Hollywood Room it was as if he was back in some Leitrim snug all over again, Jack Early recalling episodes from a twenty year-old past when they'd first come to this country on a wave of whiskey and religious zeal.

"Remember how none of us could march in step to the Legion's Spanish band when we got to Caceres that time? Not helped by bein' half-cut, mind. But then weren't we all in the same boat, landing up over here green as grass and twice as ignorant."

His face had taken on a wistful expression before another recollection came rolling out, this time when they heard Irish voices across enemy lines belonging to fellows like themselves, only fighting for the other side, and when one of their own lads hoisted up an Irish ham inviting them over for a slice, it being Christmas time, didn't the other crowd shoot it to flitters.

While Furlong recalled horrors like seeing the roaming dogs on abandoned farms feasting on human corpses, Early joked about shooting them for sniping practice, and when the Cavan men's legendary trenching skills were alluded to his own memories were of digging up shallow graves to get the coats off the dead buried there because their own operetta general had failed to provide them with any proper uniforms.

Still, as far as the man at his side was concerned, O'Duffy was Ireland's last lost leader, at one point raising a toast to their dead commander accompanied by an equally boozy salute to Franco's portrait on the far wall. Seeing the barman's face glaze over, Furlong quickly remarked, "I suppose you'll be moving on soon, then. From here, I mean?"

Early grinned.

"Ah, sure, this rolling stone here might gather some moss for a change. Anyway, it doesn't seem to have done yourself any harm, being well in, I'd say, with the right crowd."

Glancing at the bottle, he drained his glass. But before he could summon up a fresh round, excusing himself, Furlong told him, "Afraid this where I have to take my leave of you. See a man about a dog, or *perro,* as they say out here. Still, the crack's been great, going over old times like this."

Another lie. A big fat on, at that.

"Ah, sure, no matter," returned the other. "While I'm still down here what's to prevent the pair of us pickin' up where we left off, chewin' the fat till the cows come home?"

*

Leaving the hotel, Furlong walked back through the dead siesta streets to *Las Golondrinas,* and letting himself in, dropped into his chair to gaze out at his own private sector of slowly darkening sea. As well as feeling sober he'd an emptiness in his stomach which didn't come from hunger but an uneasiness higher up, and after a time he rose and from under the couch hauled out the suitcase with its cache of secrets.

At one time its darkened leather must have been a golden, yellowish tan, but when he bought it in a second-hand shop in Bedford, only a set of initials, RMT, recalled its former grandeur before ending up in the rough paws of a motorway paddy requiring a valise for his few duds. Along the way and over the years it had gathered a crop of peeling shipping-line stickers, the newest of which read, P & O Plymouth-Santander, the route he'd taken when he returned to this country, making his way south, following the sun.

The group photograph, with Early standing at the back and himself in front, lay on top of his old green and gold hurling jersey, bringing back a memory of how some of the lads brought their sticks with them, although more for weaponry than the chance of a bruising game with the Kerrymen.

He also recalled how the auxiliaries in their *tercio*, first dusky faces any of them had ever seen, were greatly taken with those same hooked hurleys, bartering for them with whatever they found on the battlefield. After a victory, the Foreign Legion granted their Moorish troops a regulation two hour's looting spree, along with another Arab custom of taking the ears of the enemy for trophies, and "Snipe" Mulligan had swapped one for a wrist-watch. But then the "Snipe" was the most fanatical of the squad by far and when not exhorting them to attend the open air field masses he was fulminating about the atrocities the Reds had perpetrated.

"I mean, did youse hear what them anarchist animals done in Cuenca? Let the lunatics out of their asylum, then gave them knives to butcher the Franciscan friars who'd been taking care of them."

The list went on. The doctor tortured on his own operating table, the nuns' heads used as footballs, the schoolmaster taken out and shot by his own pupils.

Personally, he felt there might be more to fear from the Bridegrooms of Death, as the Moors fighting alongside them were known, their pedlar followers creeping up to their lines at night with contraband liquor and tobacco and whatever else they'd stripped from the bodies of the republican dead, and before closing the lid of the suitcase he dredged up something else which might have been one of those items.

Wrapped in an old khaki sock, it still preserved the smell of the Vaseline they rubbed on their army boots. Or, in this instance, the German Luger never fired, at least not by him. Still, it was only a pistol, and not a leathery human ear buried down there at the bottom of the case.

By now the swifts outside were tracing their nightly parabolas in the sky, and snapping down the clasps on the suitcase lid, he nudged it back under the couch where it properly belonged. Out of sight. Out of mind.

A week later, then another, his old comrade in arms still hadn't moved on, hopefully out of sight and out of mind, despite Marrakesh being mentioned and deeper south, Tuareg territory, and all those indigo-clad wanderers with their camels and veiled women.

Then one night, having arranged to meet him in the hotel bar, he found Guzman sitting alongside him, Early looking like he hadn't stirred from the same stool since they'd last seen one another, still in his shorts and shirt with its lurid tropical motif.

On the other hand, this was a new Guzman, flushed of face and with a moist gleam in his eye, greeting him with a cheerful, "Come, amigo, let's all three of his drink to past campaigns and battles shared!"

"So what front was it you said you saw action on yourself?"asked Early. "Sure, you never know, mebbe the three of us were as close as we are right now and didn't know it."

Responding, Guzman uttered the one word, "Malaga", and growing bolder, Early commented, "We heard tell the fighting was real bad down there. Nearly as bad as up north where *our* lads were."

Fixing him with a bleary stare, the other growled, "We drove the scum here into the sea, then cleansed the streets of the *mierda* left behind."

"Aye, indeed, and all thanks to the big boss man himself up on that wall there and still lookin' out for us all."

Rarely had Franco, it seemed, been accorded so much openly expressed adulation in the Hollywood Room, Furlong even fearing Early might throw in a stiff-armed salute for good measure, before, rising to his feet, an unsteady Guzman headed off to the *servicios*. Watching him go, Early remarked, "If that armchair fusilier ever fired a shot in anger, I'm a feckin' Dutchman. But then *you're* a lot more familiar with him than I am. Matter of interest, what exactly *does* he do when he's not blowin' hot air?"

"He's a lot of pull and influence here, so I'd be careful about taking too many liberties with him if I were you."

"But then you're not Jack Early. Not after him riskin' life and limb for this country of theirs and still carryin' the scars to prove it."

News to Furlong, of course, knowing the other, like himself, hadn't suffered as much as a scratch in their embarrassingly short campaign together.

After Guzman still hadn't returned, Early said, "What do you think, mebbe he's lyin' in there the worse for wear. Somethin' more serious, even?"

Returned to his cheeky old self, he was grinning as he said it.

"Okay, I'll take a look," Furlong told him. "I'm due for a visit there myself anyway."

Save for one seemingly occupied cubicle, the lavatory was empty, and after doing his business at the urinals and noisily washing his hands Furlong waited for some response from behind that one closed door, but nothing broke the silence, and so to satisfy himself no one was inside, bending down, he peered under the door before leaving.

Back in the Hollywood Room Jorge gestured to him and when he went up to him at his end of the bar, leaning forward, the young waiter murmured, "Senor Guzman left by the pool-side *exito,* Senor Eugene, I think he may have been feeling unwell."

Then, even more discreetly, "May I speak privately with you about a *pocita problema* regarding your Irish friend?"

"Problem?"

"Si, the small matter of the bar-bill."

That was on a Thursday. Three days later the *problema* had escalated, as now it transpired the hotel bill was also in arrears and only allowed to remain so because of his own connection with his "Irish friend". Hoping the situation might resolve itself he stayed clear of the Hollywood Room, until one afternoon, lying dozing on the couch in his apartment, the knock he'd been dreading arrived.

Splashing water on his face and pulling on a vest and trousers, he let Early in, who greeted him with a breezy, "Well, if the mountain won't come to Mohammed . . ."

However, despite the jauntiness, it wasn't long before he showed he was as shameless as ever, explaining that he'd had a "trifling setback at the hotel regarding a temporary shortfall in the funding department, and so if you could see your way to tiding me over I'd be eternally grateful, and in the meantime mebbe I could kip down on your sofa? For old times' sake?"

It was an uncomfortable moment, but Early had no-one to blame but himself. At which point the situation took an even more alarming turn.

"Look, I've left my stuff down below. But, sure, don't worry, nobody saw me, same as at the hotel. That bloke we met, you know the one we got bevvied with? Well, he's been asking all sorts of questions about me, *you*, as well. Him and that police captain mate of his".

"Delgado? How did you meet *him*?"

"Sure, him and that Guzman fella never outa the place."

"So, how much exactly is it you owe?"

"For the room, or the bar?"

Swallowing his bile, Furlong said, "Both."

"Ah, give or take, somethin' in the region of . . ." said Early, mentioning a sum which seemed outrageous going by current Spanish rates.

"Look, if I'd anyone else to turn to I wouldn't be bothering you. Anyway, if the shoe was on the other foot, wouldn't I do the same for an old comrade myself?"

Seeing no way out of it, he'd given Early sufficient to pay off his booze bill, suspecting he might even have used his own name and reputation in the hotel to run up a tab in the first place

"Sure, I'll be outa your hair before you know it," his closing words before turning in, having the gall to enquire if there might be a drink about the place for a night-cap for the pair of them.

At some stage he must have dropped off himself, for when he awoke, Early and his old ex-army knapsack were both missing, leaving nothing behind save a slew of discarded bedding and a strong reek of the Sweet Afton he'd been smoking.

Still, if he thought he'd got shot of Jack Early by paying him off, then airing the apartment, he was mistaken, for questions still hung in the air when he returned to his old routine of that last drink at the Miramar where it was obvious Jorge was embarrassed despite never once referring to his absent "Irish friend".

Guzman and Delgado were another matter, however, suggesting all three of them should take their drinks to a corner table, and so bracing himself he waited for the interrogation to begin.

"As a matter of interest, just exactly when *was* the last time you saw Senor Early?" Delgado kicked off.

"A couple of weeks ago probably. Most of the time he preferred being on his own."

"Even though one got the impression you were a lot closer than that."

"No, we were just two people who hadn't seen one another for nearly twenty years, that's all."

At which point, Guzman said, "Yet when I spoke with him he said you'd both been through a great deal together. "Brothers under fire", were his words."

"Well, I'd hardly describe our time in the Fifth Bandera in those terms exactly."

Wondering where all this might be leading, Furlong waited for enlightenment, and when it arrived it was a shock.

"Two days ago," said Delgado, "further along the coast at Nerja, a fisherman found your friend's belongings on the beach there, a *bolsa* with some correspondence inside with his name on it."

Both were staring at him now, gauging his reaction.

Keeping his face stiff, he said, "You think he might have drowned?"

"Possibly. Was he a good swimmer, do you know?"

"I never heard him mention the pool, or saw him on the beach either."

Like most of his fellow Irish inlanders in the Bandera, Early had never learned to swim. But Furlong was already warming to the notion of him being swallowed by the waves, leaving nothing behind but his knapsack as evidence of his tragic fate, a neat and satisfactory postscript to the entire Jack

Early saga. And if at some future date a postcard arrived at *Las Golondrinas* from Marrakesh, it would only end up along with all those other buried items in the suitcase under his couch.

That encounter with Delgado and Guzman took place some months ago, and ever since they'd left him in peace. Even so, there was one routine he'd forgotten about, and one night Guzman reminded him of it.

"Dona Dolores tells me she's been missing her Irish senor's visits to her establishment of late," meaning the knocking-shop on Calle Los Nidos. "But then both of us know another may have taken hold of his affections, if not his *pico*."

Enjoying his shocked reaction, Guzman grinned, then leaning forward, confided, "All of us have been pierced by *Cupido's* darts at one time or the other, which is why I'm more than happy to offer my personal advice in this matter."

Anxious to avoid the other's scrutiny, Furlong could only stare out through the bar's rear windows at the hotel's expanse of beach, empty as always at this hour.

"So, are you agreeable to my helping you out with your *problema*, or not?"

"*Problema*?"

Guzman laughed.

"My innocent Irish friend, it's clear you're unused to the ways of women. Trust me when I say there's not one who can't be persuaded given the right kind of lure. And, anyway, why would someone like her, a widow on her own with no other means of support, turn her nose up at such a generous offer, house-keeper to a respectable, foreign senor like yourself? Take the word of one who knows, she'll be sharing your bed before you know it."

DIEGO

As soon as he hears Adriana leaving the house his own daily routine begins. Breakfast, then ten minutes of exercise, stretching, mainly, followed by reading, broken by occasional trips to his peephole to look down on the street below. Finally, writing.

In the same brand of exercise-book he was given at school, writing about his life in the barrio and his neighbours and the landowners who employed them there, forty years on his subject matter's still some of those same *falangistas*, only he's at war with them now and their blue-shirted allies in another part of the country in an olive-green military uniform of his own.

At the moment he's revisiting the winter offensive of '37 and his battalion laying siege to Teruel, but with the nationalists getting succour from the air. Lying in their trenches, he and his *companeros* are familiar by now with the high whine

91

of the enemy Fiats or the deeper growl of the Messerschmitt 109s, except this night, shivering in their holes in the ground, they hear a heavy German Junker fly overhead with yet another cargo of provisions.

Sharing his dugout was this International Brigader named Lars who liked his *conac,* and who persuaded him to creep forward into the darkness for a closer look at the enemy's airborne bounty.

Hunkered down fifty metres from the town's walls, they heard another plane pass over, again something falling from it, but, oddly this time, squawking as it fell, and recognising the cry a turkey makes, he took it for a belated Christmas offering of some sort. After seeing two more of the creatures descend, he and the Swede returned to their lines, a story soon after going the rounds that because of their weight and vertical falling power domestic fowl were now being employed by the nationalists to drop more delicate items such as medical supplies.

Sitting here now with pen and paper in front of him, an even more bizarre aerial episode comes into his head, a couple of junior pilots from a Malaga flying-club bombing their column with melons, laughing down on them from their open cockpits, and he still burns with the anger he felt that day as yet another generation of those same sons-of-bitches race past in the street below sounding their car horns, making him think of Adriana forced to endure it down there on the *costa* herself.

From what he's read, Franco may even have helped encourage some of it himself, turning a blind eye to all that excess and naked flesh displayed on the beaches there, although

Adriana avoids talking about the latter because he's still a man and with something still between his legs despite it not being put to much use of late.

Before he met her, after a night spent drinking with his friends, he would sometimes finish up at old Tia Hortensia's place at El Calvario with one of her country girls, but never being much of a cocksman anyway when he fell in love he was glad he hadn't squandered his affections in all the wrong places.

After the war ended and he sneaked back to the barrio like some haggard wraith, those first few months were the hardest to bear and often he thought of giving himself up. But Adriana was the one who was steadfast, telling him that even if he wasn't shot he'd end up in the concentration camp at Torremolinos instead. A bare, open field without barracks or latrines, it housed up to four thousand prisoners, the inmates later used as slave labour to build the landing strips for Malaga airport, now catering for all those rich foreign tourists she found herself looking after.

In the same way as he's learned to regulate his bowel movements, his eating habits have also become geared to their one evening meal together and the rest of the time he eats little, so he takes a siesta when life outside also slows to a full stop.

Lying on his narrow couch it sometimes feels as if he'll never rise from it again. Times, too, some of those same depressing half-dreams of his linger on, like today, here in a forest in Asturias, for the trees have fir cones and needles, snow on their branches, too, reminding him of Christmas when baubles dangle there. But the deeper into the wood he goes he sees these are not innocent decorations, but bodies, and this isn't some nightmare but history repeating itself, the wood real, like the corpses of those young green recruits executed as deserters by his own side and left as a warning to the rest of his battalion.

Other horrors, too, return, polluting the present. The dog roaming the battlefield with part of a human limb in its jaws, the victim sitting up in his newly dug grave and beaten to death by his killers for disturbing their lunch, the women raped, heads shaved, or both.

After he filled his first exercise-book, Adriana took an interest herself, but as another and another blue-backed volume was added to the collection, she no longer enquired about the content, and as the subject matter grew darker still he felt relieved in a way, an added safeguard being she never was able to read his handwriting anyway.

Waiting, listening for her arrival, he sometimes wonders what if some evening the key doesn't turn in the lock below, his imagination furnishing the direst of possibilities, a fall, a sudden illness, an accident in the hotel kitchens or in one of the rooms. Back and forth he paces, four steps forward, the same back, as familiar with the dimensions of his confinement as any convict in his cell before going back to writing about the past to take his mind off the even more dangerous present, and this turns out to be one of those worrying days, making him stiffen, ears tuned to a conversation taking place in the street below.

Even inside his thick-walled space it still feels like one of the hottest days of the year. Clad in nothing but a vest and a pair of cotton shorts, trying to keep the sweat from falling on to the paper in front of him, he's been travelling back in time and place to when the war looked as if it already had been won, and in the streets of Barcelona everywhere could be heard the whirring of a thousand liberated sewing-machines taken from the pawnshops and returned to their owners by decree of the republic.

Wrenched brutally back to the present, hearing the hoarse tones of the old harridan opposite, his blood runs cold.

"She's never seen during the day, but if one's up early enough you might catch sight of her leaving the house then returning home late at night. You could, of course, always enquire for her at her place of employment."

"Oh? And where might that be?"

Which, finally, is when he recognises the Crab's presence, for who else is it but that same son of a bitch returned to pry and torture.

"Some people say they've seen her in that big new hotel on the costa."

"She has a position there?"

"If you care to call it by that name. Still, who cares what some old *pensionista* thinks?"

"Where you're very much mistaken, and why it's my privilege to be speaking with you here today, senora."

"You, also, Senor Guzman."

"You know who I am?"

"Here in the barrio we're proud of how you've become such a fine caballero with all your important new friends."

"No man should never forget where he comes from. Still, may I request one small favour of you to keep this conversation a private matter just between the two of us?"

"Certainly, you may, as well as any other information that might come my way."

Pressed to the window, he listened to his old enemy's footsteps fade away, and after a time, steeling himself, he peered out to see if the old *bruja* herself was still there, but the doorstep was bare like the street itself.

At some point he lay down, but when he closed his eyes even one of those worrying four o'clock dreams of his would have been a relief. They, at least, belonged to the past, for why had Guzman pretended he hadn't known Adriana worked at the Miramar? Unless, of course, he was simply following his nose like some cur sniffing the air? Still, thinking of him as canine instead of crustacean didn't help, even if it was something to joke about with Adriana later, although any laughter would have to be hers in case the neighbours heard a male voice from the grave joining in.

However, the wireless was always there to provide cover as people kept their ears cocked to what others might be listening to as well, including on their gramophones, even though Adriana had destroyed all their old records just as she'd burned their family photographs when the police came asking for a likeness of her absent *rojo* of a husband that time.

At some point he must have dozed off, the church bells waking him, six slow-paced peals, and then he heard their radio playing below what sounded like a tango medley, and when he went down her back was turned, and crossing to the radio reducing the volume, he saw her stiffen."

"Please can we keep the radio on? I like listening to it while we're eating."

"For company, you mean?"

That was petty of him, he realised.

The music had reverted to their own flamenco rhythms now, and after an interval the announcer read out a short news bulletin about Franco's recent medical operation, although not as life threatening as Diego would have liked.

Rising from the table, Adriana carried her own plate over to the sink while he sat finishing what he could of the *paella* in the dish in front of him. Then, as though still far too exhausted to speak, she went up the stairs to their bedroom while he stayed where he was visualising her undressing above, then bathing her hands and face, something she did each night before he came up himself, sliding in alongside her, breathing in the scent of her cologne under the covers.

All the while the radio still warbled on, and finishing the wine in the carafe, he went to the cupboard, taking down another.

It's been a long time since he's allowed himself get drunk in this way, the *tinto* already easing away some of the ache inside. But then why shouldn't he be like other men for once? Here in the dark on his own like this he's thinking of the *gitano* he hears coming back singing in the small hours, and he envies that gypsy, free to feel the night air on his face, head full of foolish, unrealisable dreams.

Reaching for the carafe, his hand knocks it from the table, the resulting detonation on the tiles at his feet causing him to freeze. Then, after a moment or so, he makes for the stairs, determined to have it out with her, for a man shouldn't be disregarded in this way no matter how many jugs of wine he overturns, and reaching the bedroom, he stands listening to the rise and fall of her breathing there in the dark.

Peeling off his clothes and groping his way across to their bed, he slides in alongside this stranger lying unmoving there, until unable to help himself, he whispers, "Are you awake?" and getting no reply, "What's the matter? What is it?" hearing her finally murmur, "Nothing. I just need my rest, even if you don't."

"What's that supposed to mean?"

"I'm just tired, that's all."

"Unlike me, you mean? Is that it? Well?"

Unable to let things go, he's sitting up in bed now, glaring at the shadowy outline of her head on the pillow for, tipsy, as he is, he's convinced something must have happened before she entered the house this evening to contaminate the very air between them.

"Don't treat me this way, you hear? Damn it, answer me!"

Worryingly for them both his voice has become raised, and suddenly he feels her hand reaching out to cover his mouth, the sobering touch and scent of her like that bringing him back to his senses.

"Drink doesn't suit you," he hears her whisper. "It also makes people talk in their sleep."

Then her hand withdraws, and back on his own side of the bed once more, waiting for sleep to catch up, he lies listening for her to drift off first.

JOHNNIE

Sand had gotten into his shoes, and taking them off and slapping the soles together, it strikes him just when was the last time he'd waded in the ocean anyway, so rolling up the cuffs of his slacks, in he goes, gazing out to where a flotilla of *feria* craft's still bobbing about out there.

A light breeze is coming off the sea making his feet feel cold, and maybe it *is* being in the water but he's thinking about that buddy of Furlong's and that fake suicide of his, that's if it *was* phoney after all, and even though he realises he's just being plain morbid now he wonders how the headlines would read if ever he felt the urge himself.

Presumably those hacks back home would only write he'd been on this slow-burn regime of self-harm anyway, and just then having helped rough out his own obituary, he laughs, until realising he's no longer alone, he sees young Jorge from the Miramar standing on the beach behind him holding his loafers in his hand.

"On nights like these, Senor Johnnie, people are abroad who might be tempted to steal these fine American *zabatos* of yours."

And not necessarily this evening, either, he feels like telling him, before slipping the shoes back on again while Jorge watches, dressed to kill in honour of the occasion, dazzling white shirt, razor-pleated slacks, greased back hair in an Elvis pompadour.

"May I be permitted to be the one to buy *you* a *copa* for once, Senor Johnnie?"

He's always liked the kid, and seeing and hearing him in this mood, playful, yet respectful still, he caves in, having no real plans anyway.

However, instead of heading back up to where the evening *paseo's* now in full swing, Jorge leads him along the playa towards the hotel, where, padding past in the dark, they hear the muzak coming through the open beach-front windows from the bar inside.

Just about here where the hotel's private beach merges into the public one, Johnnie comes to a halt, for this was where Delgado brought him down to see where he'd been mugged and later his belongings recovered.

"Is something the matter, Senor Johnnie?" Jorge asks.

"No, just taking a breather, that's all. This place you have in mind, much further, is it?"

"Only a little way, you'll see."

Not that he's able to, for away from the glare of the town he's already beginning to feel as though he's stepped into territory that's alien, dangerous, even.

"Do you want to turn back, Senor Johnnie?"

"No, no, keep on going."

Which is when he hears what sounds like the stuttering beat of a generator, spotting a string of lights up ahead looped through the fronds of a palm tree outside one of those beach bars they call *chiringuitos* here.

Up close the place comes across as even more of a dump. Still, he's been in far worse places and looks forward to that first long drink, possibly a *mojito*, for it's like the sort of joint he knows from Havana, the music he can hear sounding Latin as well, his professional ear picking up what can only be the mambo beat of Perez Prado.

Drawing aside the flimsy raffia curtain hanging in the doorway, Jorge ushers him inside, the dimensions oughly those of someone's living-room, ceiling, bamboo, floor, beaten earth, with a basic zinc-topped bar running along one wall, the clientele a dozen or so of the usual washed up drifter types presided over by this six-foot, dread-locked black guy who seems to have been expecting them.

"Welcome to Howie's, *muchachos*. I trust you to see it, Jorge, our honoured guest's provided with his own personal poison."

The music's still playing, still Latin, coming from this beat-up old phonograph in the corner, a stack of discs piled alongside, and speculating whether any of his own might actually be among them he watches the stylus reach the end of its groove, the arm lifting then going back to the start again of that early fifties cha-cha hit, "Patricia".

He's detecting a distinct whiff of weed now, Howie having a big fat reefer of his own smouldering in an ash-tray in front of him, Jorge returning with a glass of something tall and amber-tinted along with a bottle of beer he assumes for himself and announcing, "I got Senor Howie to mix you one of his famous *especials* himself."

Freighted with ice and a hefty floating slice of lime, it tastes pretty close to a perfect highball, and when he nods his appreciation, the kid confides, "Senor Howie's an Americano also."

"Woulda said closer to Freetown or Kingston myself."

No females appear present, so when one now emerges from the kitchen out back he does a discreet double-take. In denim hip-huggers and a skin-tight Jack Daniel's tee shirt, blonde, blue-eyed, she's definitely stacked, coming straight across to their table and setting down a plate of those little *empanada* things.

"It's our privilege to serve you, Senor Ray. Everything is on the house."

Her accent has a Nordic inflection, possibly Swedish, but close-up she's not nearly as young as he first thought, but a looker, still.

"What's your name, honey?"

"Annika," she tells him, giving him this big white-toothed smile, and after she's left, Jorge confides, "Senorita Annika's an *artista*," indicating a bunch of pictures hanging back of the bar."

All appear to be portraits of sad-eyed clowns, but not bad, either, and so if he downs a few more of Howie's lethal *especials* he might find himself waking up in his hotel room, billfold a lot lighter, stuck with some mournful looking Coco character staring down at him from the wall, not that he's any intention of getting wasted.

Jorge, however, is well into his second, or is it his third

cerveza? Lying back in his chair, he has this big grin on his face, and so he asks him, "Come here a lot, do you?"

"Not as often as Senor Furlong. I told him he might meet with you and I here this evening."

Moments later Howie comes across, pulling up a chair for himself.

"Jorge tells me you're staying at the Miramar. I trust you intend spending some time with us down here, or are you just passing through?"

"Sorta undecided at the moment."

"Well, whatever you do decide, tonight you're our guest of honour."

After he'd gone back to the bar, Jorge says, "Senor Howie's *chiringuito* was the first one to open here and still the most *popular.*"

"Even though not too many locals seem to patronise the place. Yourself excluded, of course."

The kid grinned.

"I intend making my way to your own great country one day, Senor Johnnie, so I wish to find out as much as I can about your people and their customs before I go."

"But why do you think so many of them are down here instead of back home?"

"*Sol,* sea, plus your American dollar goes a long way."

"So what about me? Why do you think *I'm* here?"

The kid stares hard at the bottle on the table in front of him.

"You and Senor Furlong are not like these people. You have your own private reasons for being here."

Someone new has just now entered the place and is talking confidentially with Howie up at the bar, Annika appearing to take on board what he has to say seriously herself, shooting nervous glances over at the curtained doorway, some of that same uneasiness being picked up by Jorge.

"Shall we make our way back to the hotel now, Senor Johnnie?"

"But didn't you say you were off-duty tonight?"

"Si, but it's getting late and it will be much safer if you and I return there together."

"For you, or for me?"

He realises he's being a real ass-hole, but then everywhere he goes here people seem to be pussy-footing around him a lot of the time.

"Come on, whaddya say? One more for the road? For the Virgen?"

However, it's clear the other's no longer in the mood, announcing, "I need to use the *servicios*."

After he's been gone some considerable time it strikes Johnnie he's been away longer than seems normal, so could the kid have run out on him leaving him to make his way back to the Miramar on his own after all? Gazing about him, the atmosphere in the place appears to be far less relaxed and friendly as well, some sort of council of war taking place up at the bar seemingly sparked off by the young guy who'd arrived earlier, and so draining his glass he decides it's time for him to bail out and call it a day.

Moments later, however, raised voices can be heard outside, that young hippy crowd he'd been fraternising on the beach with earlier bursting in, the girl weeping, the ringleader guy in the sheepskin coat yelling, "They've arrested Leon, man!

Busted him just because he's black! Fucking fascist pigs, they think they can get away with murder!"

Spooked by that one word "murder", the girl—*what's her name again? Rusty, is it?*—drops full-length on the floor, everyone staring at her lying there.

"You gotta do something, man, you hear?"

However, nothing's capable of shifting the stony look on Howie's handsome Negro face, not even when, "Shit, man, we're *American*, for fuck's sake!" rings out.

Spotting him sitting over in the corner on his own, the young guy cries, "They won't fuck with *you*, man, they'll listen to *you*! That Nazi cop captain says he's gonna round up everyone looks like Jesus Christ!"

Coming around from behind the bar, Howie crosses to Rusty, still on the floor, still sobbing, and lifting her up, limp as a rag, he lays her out on a chair, while huddled in the doorway her companions look on like the bunch of scared schoolkids they truly are by now.

"Just what the hell happened, anyway? You musta done somethin'".

"Took a dip in the ocean, that's all. Where's the crime in that?"

"In your birthday suits, I suppose?"

"That ain't the point. They can't just run people outa town because of the length of their hair, right? Or throw 'em in the slammer because of the fucking color of their skin."

This time the silence in the place is practically deafening, no one daring to look anywhere near their host.

So far Johnnie's been strictly on the fence, but he's beginning to feel a renewed sense of kinship with these young

innocents abroad, not just because of the color of their passports, but because not so long ago skinny-dipping off some
foreign beach somewhere would have seemed like a terrific
idea to someone like him.

Next moment, thrusting an anxious face through the
hanging fronds in the doorway, Jorge appears on the scene,
Howie greeting him, "Don't look so worried, *muchacho*, your
famous friend here's still all in one piece," and making his way
across to his table, the kid murmurs, "The *policia* are on their
way here. Forget these people, Senor Johnnie, they've only
themselves to blame for their conduct."

"Like taking a swim as nature intended?"

"No, being disrespectful of the Virgen. Especially that one
in the overcoat."

"Then, I guess, he deserves everything that's coming to him."

Except that the same Mister Big-Mouth still didn't seem
to have got the message, shouting, "Goddammit, we're all
American citizens! Times like these, we *gotta* stick together!"

"Like back home, you mean?" Howie tells him. "Look, this
is a bar I run here, not some foreign fucking embassy, so you
and your pals should hightail it outa here before we *all* end
up in the slammer."

Coming round, the girl pipes up, "He's right, listen to him.
We should move on like he says. Tarifa? Right?"

"Fuck Tarifa, what about Leon? Or have you forgotten he's
banged up in some local lock-up right now?"

"We don't know that. Mebbe they'll let him out in the
morning, and he can catch up with us."

This entire debate's sounding like it's gone into slow-motion
now, Johnnie wondering just what Leon had done to get

106

himself busted anyway, whereas Howie doesn't seem sympathetic in the slightest.

"Look, I don't give a rat's ass what you do, or don't do, long as you take your shit outa here. Got any sense left, you'll start making yourselves scarce while you still got the chance."

"Except that, regretfully, it may be just a little bit late for that."

The interjection's come from the back of the place, but while everyone else has turned round, Johnnie recognises the voice only too well.

Instead of being rigged out in his customary police captain's uniform, Delgado's looking civilian sharp in an expensive suit, silk shirt, patterned necktie, despite the jacket left unbuttoned to reveal the regulation firearm strapped to his belt.

Clicking his fingers, summoning two of his men, one taking up position at the rear, the other at the door, straight off he addresses the girl.

"Following an inspection of your passports, you and your companions, senorita, are at liberty to go. However, if you haven't gone from the immediate vicinity in the next half-hour you will all be taken into custody and re-united with your negro friend in the much less pleasant surroundings of the Torremolinos *comisaria*."

"But what's he been charged with? What's he supposed to've *done*?" protests Sheepskin Coat.

"I can, if you wish, arrange for a visit and he can tell you himself. However, you should know the charge is insulting the national flag which is a serious offence. At least, in this country, it is. *Passportes, por favor*."

The young hippies start fumbling for them, the cop at the

door collecting and finally handing them to his superior who only cursorily leafs through the blue-backed bundle.

One, however, he retains, turning its pages, Sheepskin Coat nervously staring at it in his hand, until, humiliatingly, Delgado gestures for him to come forward to retrieve it, and moments later he and his little beaten posse file silently out into the night.

After they've gone nothing can be heard but the record scratching to the end of yet another cycle, until, taking another disc from the pile, Annika threads it on the spindle, a piano intro crackling forth followed by his rendering of "All Of Me". Sitting there hearing his own voice like that he wonders if Sheepskin Coat and his young friends out there are listening to it as well, until wrenched back to reality he realises Delgado's now standing just feet away.

"It would appear you have the unfortunate habit of ending up, my American *amigo*, in the company of the wrong people in the wrong place. Frankly, it's not wise consorting with those who bring their ugly habits with them and give their own country and your own a bad name."

"But, Senor Capitan," protests Jorge, "Senor Ray and I were here long before these other young Americanos arrived."

"*Camarero*, be good enough to mind your manners as well as your place and fetch a *conac* for myself and whatever my friend here himself is having," and rising, the kid goes to the bar, and Johnnie sees there are tears in his eyes.

"So, tell me," Delgado says, sitting down, "were you impressed by our little annual celebration earlier? Or, like your fellow compatriots who've just now left us, you have no time for such occasions."

"I wouldn't say that."

"So, you *are* a religious man, then."

"I wouldn't say that either."

"Even though some of your recordings are in that vein?" He smiled.

"Don't look so surprised. In a small community like ours it's important to check out, as you Americans say, those visiting our shores. Even someone as illustrious as yourself."

Then, leaning forward, he confided, "Senor Ray, this is not the sort of place to socialise in even if those present speak the same language. Permit my men to escort you back to the hotel. After all, we wouldn't wish for a repetition of that little misadventure of yours of some nights ago."

"Thanks for the offer, but I'm sure Jorge's perfectly capable of accompanying me when it's time to leave."

"Very well, have it your way. But perhaps I can persuade you to join Senor Guzman and myself at our usual meeting-place a little later on."

After he and his two uniformed goons had gone, the kid says, "Shall we go ourselves now? I know another safer way we can take, Senor Johnnie."

"Without bumping into the captain, you mean? You don't much care for him and his friends, do you?"

Jorge stared at him. Then, gulping down the *conac* he'd brought for Delgado, he sat down staring at the drained glass now in front of him.

"When our civil war ended, Senor Johnnie, I was two years old, and although to some it might seem a long time ago Capitan Delgado and those like him still enjoy reminding others what it was like to be on the losing side."

Pausing, he runs a finger around the rim of the empty brandy glass.

"But then many people wish to forget what happened to them then. Two of my uncles were killed, a second cousin, also, yet I had to find out about it from a neighbour when he was drunk, and afterwards he avoided the topic, just as I did, for I've no wish to make enemies of those who might lose me my job."

"Like the captain, you mean?"

"All he has to say is the word and Don Gustavo will let me go."

"But why when you're the best bartender the Miramar has. Everyone knows that. Even Don Gustavo."

"Just two weeks ago he dismissed his head housekeeper, Senora Adriana. She, too, was *excepcional*."

"But, again, why?

"Some say a private matter between them. Others say Señor Guzman may have had a hand in it."

"The captain's friend?"

"Si, because of her dead husband, who people say was a *rojo*, a red."

"So some people never forget."

"In our country, Senor Johnnie, no one forgets, not even those who don't remember."

"Anyway, this housekeeper, what's going to happen to her now?"

"End her days in the barrio like all those other women who lost their husbands."

"While the rest of us lie in the sun, drink and grow fat?"

"But you yourself do none of those things, Senor Johnnie."

"What about what's here in the glass in front of me?"

Yet even that's not enough to lift the kid from his gloom, so he tells him, "How about I talk to Don Gustavo and put in a good word for you?"

"You would do that for me, Senor Johnnie?"

"Why not? Somebody's gotta stand up and tell these assholes where to get off."

And despite the bar-room bluster, he means it for once.

"Anyway, let's get outa here, you're right. We've had more than enough excitement for one night."

"But what about Senor Furlong? I told him he could meet us here after he's been to mass."

"Never had *him* tagged as the religious sort."

"No, but the *irlandese* also are Catholic like the Spanish."

The dilemma, of course, now is whether to order a fresh round or not, but before he can make up his mind, the individual they've been discussing just then himself appears in the doorway.

Furlong's smiling, hand outstretched, Johnnie greeting him with, "You just missed all the fun."

"Them young ones and that carry-on of theirs in the water, you mean?"

"In here, too."

"Outraging public decency on terra firma as well, were they?"

"Fully clothed this time. That's after Captain Delgado showed up, of course."

"Well, aside from all of that, are we going to have a jar here or not? It's not every day the Good Lady Herself takes to the waves. Water and wine, wine and water, it's in the good book."

"No, this joint's got a jinx on it, let's go some place else."

"The hotel?"

"Helping Herr Capitan and his good buddy Guzman celebrate seeing off the skinny-dippers?"

Furlong laughed.

"We used to swim in our bare pelts back home ourselves."

Then he says, "So, Guzman was here as well, was he?"

"If not in the flesh, most definitely in spirit."

"On the subject of spirits, I've a bottle at my place. That's if you don't mind a thirty-year old John J."

On the way there, it occurs to Johnnie their route seems to take a lot longer than the one coming here, but he's relishing the coolness of the night air after the place they've just left. All along the front the celebrations are still going on, but here where Furlong is now leading them the streets are deserted, an occasional cat scooting off at their approach, and already the little white painted houses have their shutters up and everywhere there's that heavy night-time scent of jasmine and mimosa.

Finally, reaching a low-rise apartment block set in back from the street, Furlong announces, "Home sweet home," but as he's busy searching for his keys, Jorge announces, "Here I must bid you both *buenas noches senores*."

"Absoluutely sure you are now you won't join us for that one last drink?"

"No, Senor Furlong, Ignacio the relief barman comes off duty at two."

As he spoke the distant double chiming of a church bell could be heard.

"Well, another time then. And if you *do* happen to run into the captain and his good friend Senor Guzman be certain to pass on our very fondest regards."

Even though it's clearly mischievous, Jorge's face registers otherwise, and feeling sorry for the kid, Johnnie says, "Look, I'll make certain to have that chat with Don Gustavo you and I were discussing earlier."

"*Muchas gracias*, Senor Johnnie. Will you be able to find your way back to the hotel on your own?"

"Leave that to me, young Jorge," Furlong tells him. "I'll make that *my* responsibility."

Inside, anticipating a typical, dyed in the wool bachelor's residence, Johnnie's surprised by the stuffy, almost sedate nature of the apartment itself. Heavy dark furniture, even old-fashioned antimacassars draped over the backs of the chairs, reminiscent of airless Sabbath sitting-rooms and parlours he remembers from back home. Save for the pictures on the walls, of course, all of serious looking Spanish couples, the men moustachioed, the womenfolk with their obligatory mantillas and pleated paper fans.

"Make yourself easy while I rustle up some refreshments," says Furlong going into the other room, Johnnie dropping into the *salon's* only armchair, and after a brief interval his host returns with the promised whiskey bottle, a water jug and two glasses, pouring them both a couple of stiff ones.

"I took the place just as you see it when I first moved in. To tell you the truth, I couldn't be bothered changing a thing. But then I've always been something of a light traveller, a bit like yourself, I imagine."

113

The liquor has a soft peaty kick to it, but it goes down easily enough, and sinking deeper into his host's one old scuffed leather armchair, Johnnie sits back allowing the other to talk.

"Still, it'll be a lot more respectable looking when a certain senora puts her stamp on things. Maybe you came across her? Had a position in the hotel up until a while ago, but now she's been persuaded to tend to the needs of this oul' bachelor here and everything you see about you."

"Don Gustavo's head housekeeper, you mean?"

"So, you *do* know her, then?"

"No, just that Jorge happened to mention something."

"Oh? He did, did he?"

Suddenly the atmosphere had changed to something a lot less amiable.

"Just that Guzman might have had a hand in it. Her leaving the hotel, I mean."

"Feckin' Luis Casares, eh? Shoulda known *he'd* put his oar in, him and that rozzer pal of his. My mistake was letting the pair of them getting wind of my past, not that I was in much of a position to stop them finding out even if I'd wanted to . . . But, here, hang on, I want to show you something."

Going into the other room, he could be heard rooting about inside, with Johnnie sitting there expecting some sort of a revelation. However, when the mysterious object *was* revealed, it proved to be nothing other than a framed photograph which Furlong solemnly handed to him.

"That's me, there, see? Front row. Second from the left."

"So you were in the British army? World War Two?"

Furlong laughed.

"No, another little dust-up entirely, and over here, me and

all those other young buckos in that photo hell-bent on protecting the Faith and Fatherland from the Reds."

"You and our friend Guzman fought on the same side together?"

Furlong gave another laugh.

"Hardly, in *his* case. Summer soldiers, we used to call them. Fired off a coupla rounds, then back home for a feed and a furlough like it was a bank holiday weekend."

"And *this* was what brought you back?" said Johnnie, indicating the photograph. "To recapture something."

"Naw, sure, I could never settle. Kept movin' on until I ended up down here. But it looks as if I might have got myself settled now, for there's nothing like a female touch about the place to give a bloke a fresh perspective on things."

Having ended up in some sort of conversational cul-de-sac, there they sat, until finally Johnnie enquired, "You went to church this evening, Jorge tells me."

"Sure, it's only one night in the year, more for the spectacle than anythin' else. Although, when I first came out here, I'd occasionally dip a finger in the font for old time's sake, but soon lapsed, as they say . . . So, we're back to religion, are we?"

"Not really. Only I was wondering . . ."

"About what exactly?"

"Well, this here, as a matter of fact."

Taking out the little metal oval he's been carrying around with him in his pocket, he passes it over to Furlong who cups it in his palm, staring at it.

"How did you get hold of this?"

"It's some kind of religious medal, I take it?"

"That's right. What they call a *nombre de eucharistia*, given

115

to a girl on her first communion. Here, see what it says on the back?"

The light's not great, but peering at the tiny inscription, which hadn't really registered with him before, Johnnie spells out the name etched there.

"Adriana . . . Which means, I suppose, it could really belong to any number of women with that name."

"No. Just the one, because of the date."

Furlong's staring hard at him now as though expecting him to come up with something more. Something incriminating, he can't help thinking.

"Look, the truth is I just happened to find it in the street. Whoever it was, I reckon she might have dropped it at the *feria*."

The lie had slipped out a little too easily.

"To be frank, I don't even know why I held on to it, more your kinda thing, I guess. Anyway, why don't *you* have it?"

After it had changed hands, rising to his feet, Johnnie yawned.

"Reckon it's time for me to make tracks and say *muchas gracias* for all your generous hospitality this evening."

"You're certain you're okay about gettin' back to the Miramar under your own steam?"

"No, no, I'm good. No need for you to get up, I can see myself out. Take it easy, you hear? See you around . . ."

In the street outside the near deathly hush still hangs heavy in the air even though inside his own head his thoughts seem roaring away loud enough to be overheard, and all to do with this Adriana dame he's now convinced had to have been the one in his hotel room that night. Let's face it, only she could have hung the Do Not Disturb sign on the door handle after leaving her *nombre de eucharista* inside.

But then the big question arises, what exactly took place there before she left? The answer's still a blank, so then there's that next question, could he have been *that* plastered? Looking back, of course, he must have been, for hangovers of that subsequent ferocity don't usually lie.

Closer to the hotel now, and recalling how the man he'd just left in his apartment back there had talked of her in that way, has him now wondering if Furlong mightn't have been the one slipping in between the sheets there himself.

ADRIANA

Don Gustavo could always be found in his office, so when she went back to hand in her uniform she knew he would have to see her, and spotting the bundle she was carrying, he said, "There was no need to come all this way, Adriana, just to return any remaining hotel property. You could, at least, have held on to the shoes and the stockings."

However, she knew she couldn't go back to the barrio and face the one dependent on her there without putting herself through this final humiliation.

"May I speak privately with you, Don Gustavo, a moment only?"

She could see him glancing at the telephone willing it to ring, until, sighing, he said, "Everyone here at the Miramar holds you in the utmost regard, but when some of our most respected and valued patrons complained that the reputation of the hotel might be harmed because of your late husband's political history, surely you must understand only one option, painful, as it was, was left open to me."

"These "respected patrons", they have names?"

That was bold of her, foolhardy, too. But then what had she to lose?

"Might one be a certain Senor Guzman by chance?"

"Possibly so, although you might be surprised to learn he still has your best interests at heart."

Clicking his fingers, he summoned one of the young waiters hovering in the lobby area to fetch them two café *neros*.

Closing the door, oozing sincerity, Don Gustavo laid his palms flat on his desk, nothing marring its polished surface save an open leather-bound ledger and, curiously enough, one of those little souvenir globe creations, causing her to wonder if he ever actually shook it to remind him of snowy winters back in his native city, for she could make out the word *Madrid* etched in the domed glass.

On the wall behind her hung the obligatory portrait of Frank the Frog himself, the military sash he wore in all such photographs constricting his plump little womanly belly, and sitting there she could almost feel those black button eyes boring into the nape of her neck.

"When he first was made aware of your situation, Don Guzman's words were, and her I quote, but what will now become of the poor senora with no man at home to support her? But then I told him you were still this fine strong figure of a woman, better preserved than many half her age."

At this point the young waiter appeared with the heavy silver crested coffee-pot Don Gustavo himself favoured, so she thought of Carlotta's own old smoked cafetiere the pair of them took their own morning coffee from together, and seeing him pour she wondered if he'd return with a tasty crumb of gossip for those in the kitchens to savour and chew over.

After the waiter had left with the tray, Don Gustavo picked up his little glass globe, and watching, she waited to see if he might conjure up a snow-storm in miniature of his own after all, until setting it down, he said, "An acquaintance of Senor Guzman's requires someone to clean and generally take charge of his domestic affairs, and is prepared to pay a reasonable wage to a mature person with experience and discretion."

He paused to observe the effect of his words, but she was still visualising fluffy white flakes falling silently on a city she herself could only imagine but where Diego had once fought himself.

"Naturally such duties would be different from what you've been used to, but let's be realistic, someone in your situation is in no position to pick and choose."

He was gazing intently at her over steepled hands as he spoke, but even though she could see he was expecting a reply the words wouldn't come and she saw his mood change to one of chilly officialdom.

"Very well, now that you've heard all I've got to say on the subject, these here are the senor's relevant details."

Pulling out a desk drawer, he produced a slip of paper, and for an instant she thought he might be about to ask her if she wanted him to read it for her as some additional form of humiliation.

After being officially dismissed, for that's what it felt like, she stepped into the lobby now showing signs of activity because of the motor coach she could see outside, a German party already starting to disembark, elderly and with that same closed look on their faces as though preparing themselves for the worst. Their luggage was being hauled from the underbelly of the bus by three young waiters all wearing the same glued on smile hopefully oiling the way to a generous tip.

Not so long ago *she* would have been the guardian of those same suitcases after they'd been carried up to the rooms and their contents stowed away and hung in the wardrobes or arranged on the glass shelves in the bathrooms, but now that would never concern her again.

She still hadn't time to weigh up her new situation, its consequences, neither. Those would become clearer after putting on a brave face for the man waiting back in 15 Calle El Capitano for news of the world beyond his walled-in cubbyhole, except now she'd have to spin additional webs of deceit, telling him her hotel hours and duties had been changed and she'd no longer have to leave the house at such an ungodly hour. Making it worse, of course, would be his acceptance of the lie, sitting there, head buried in one of the foreign periodicals she rescued from the hotel's waste paper bins, something else she'd have to explain away. No more newspapers. No more leftovers from Carlotta's larder, either.

One of the tourists from the bus, this heavily built blonde woman in a tweed two-piece suit despite the outside temperature, was ordering the waiters about in harshly accented Spanish.

"Where is the manager, why is *he* not here?"

Then, spotting her, "You, yes, you there! Are *you* in charge here?"

Yet even though it would have been satisfying to tell this fat foreign creature where to get off, instead, she replied, "Don Gustavo will be along presently to ensure your stay with us is to your utmost comfort and satisfaction."

After she said it she saw one of the waiters staring at her, a look of awe on his young face, and approaching, he murmured, "I feel sure Senora Carlotta would have wished to say a proper adios herself to you, Dona Adriana."

She saw it was Pepe who'd blurted out her name when she'd answered Don Gustavo's telephone that time.

Lying, she told him, "Carlotta and I have already made our farewells. But you mustn't neglect your duties. It doesn't look good leaving the guests' belongings unattended in this way."

"Anyway, I won't be working here much longer. I've a relative in a place they call Baltimore in America and I intend joining him there. I've no wish to rot and grow old in the barrio like all the other *ancianos* there."

Then, face quickly changing expression, he said, "Not that you, Dona Adriana, could be ever like one of those, for you're like the Virgen Herself, forever young, having drunk from the well of youth."

Retracing her route back along the beach in daylight instead of at night after work felt unsettling as though she'd no right to be here, until once she saw someone coming towards her, a woman like herself, eyes lowered to the bleached sea-drift along the shoreline, foraging for shells washed up by the tide, and not wishing to be seen, she'd veered off inland.

The rest of the day she couldn't stop thinking about her, asking herself how long might it be before she'd be joining her, like those other scavengers searching through the bins and trash buckets behind the hotel, turning their eyes on her like so many human cats as she edged past in the shadows. As the light faded her own mood darkened as well, so by the time she reached the pueblo she felt like the woman on the shore must feel, returning after another fruitless day trudging along, eyes fixed on the sand beneath brown bare feet.

Diego, when she let herself in, was still above, which suited her, needing time to put normal expression on her face. Some chick peas and chorizo had been left over from last evening's supper, enough to put together another meal for them both, and after laying the table she listened for the sound of his felt slippers on the stairs, and when eventually he appeared and sat down, both faced one another like a couple much too tired to talk after another hard day's toil.

Watching him push the food about his plate, she felt the silence grow, until sighing, he said, "I've run out of ink. And could you get me some exercise-books as well?"

Angered, in spite of herself, she felt like snapping back, *and how about a bottle of cognac and a box of expensive Cubana cigars while I'm at it?*

However, biting back the words, she poured some more wine for them both, for what was the point of expecting him to understand even if she did manage to summon up the courage to tell him the truth? Observing him toying with his food, suddenly she had this depressing feeling they'd somehow now changed from husband and wife to mother and child.

"Well? Have you finished?" she heard herself ask, and without replying he stared at her through his spectacles held together with glue and tape, making him look older than he was, and recalling her encounter in Don Gustavo's office she was thinking of the snow globe again, that tiny enclosed world just like Diego's, with its imprisoned little mannikin inside patiently waiting for the air to turn white.

After washing and drying their two plates, she wiped the table clean while he sat picking his teeth with a matchstick just like any other normal husband in the barrio. With the radio providing its necessary background cover, it should have been the time for their usual small talk, sharing the events of their day. But not this evening, and unable to bear the silence a minute longer, rising, yawning, she told him, "I think I'll turn in. It's been a long day," and to her great relief, he replied, "Very well. I'll try not to wake you when I come up myself."

The *cama matrimonial* they shared was the one she'd saved up for and bought with her own money when they first set up home together, that being the custom of the barrio, although Diego believed the ritual outdated and at odds with progressive socialist ideals of equality between the sexes. However, *she* loved its ornate carved headboard and solid oak frame, as reassuring as some securely anchored raft in that upstairs bedroom of theirs, and at the start, afloat on it, they made love like any other normal couple right up until the time he went off to fight, returning to hide himself away like some nervous ghost in that tiny, false-walled sanctuary of his.

Lying over on her own side of the bed, sleep seems a long way off, so she turns her mind instead to an inventory of what's in their larder below, enough to see them through another month, perhaps a few more. A smallish stock of chick peas, beans, lentils, some tins of sardines, tomatoes, plus, of course, the usual day-old bread for gazpacho, finally calculating in her head how much *dinero* she's managed to put away, again the amount scarcely sufficient to keep hunger at bay.

After a time, her worry increasing, rising out of bed, she tries to remember where she's left her bag, having brought it upstairs with her instead of leaving it in the kitchen below as usual. The bag, still containing the shoes and dark stockings from the Miramar, is on a chair by the window, and feeling her way across to it and sliding a hand inside she finds the small square of paper Don Gustavo gave her, holding it up to the sliver of light coming in from the street outside.

In Don Gustavo's neat hand, the single line is nothing more than an address with no accompanying name as though intended to humiliate her even further if ever she does decide to turn up at the door unannounced. But does it really have to come to that? Is she already that desperate?

Here now in the dark, however, she has the feeling the actual moment might not be so very far off, and instead of tearing it up as she'd earlier intended she puts the scrap of paper back in the bag again, even though she's already memorised the words written there.

EUGENE

After the Day Of The Virgen everything seemed to slow down and despite it being the wrong month he felt in some sort of Lenten retreat himself, holed up in his apartment, recalling what the parish priest back home used to refer to as the sins of commission as well as omission.

Father Dowd, fresh from the seminary, and slippery as the oil of unction itself, and possibly a monsignor now, hadn't been present with those other clerics on Galway Quay to bless him and his comrades that day, and when his Bishop announced that for every Red you killed it meant a year less in Purgatory, Father Dowd said neither yea nor nay.

Six months later, when they all came back in one piece, the mood was very different, everybody who stayed behind having been badly let down it seemed, and when he went to make his first confession he rolled out the usual litany of minor transgressions when what he really needed getting off his chest were some of the terrible things he'd witnessed and been party to over there.

But Father Dowd had no wish to hear any of that despite it being filtered through a fretted wooden screen, and it turned out to be the last time he found himself in one of those same clerical sentry-boxes, either at home or here with all the old Spanish biddies lining up to unburden themselves to the perpetually unshaven, boozy Father Ignacio rumoured to be having carnal relations with his housekeeper.

An arrangement such as that, of course, was something he himself was in no position to judge or criticise that's if Guzman had anything to do with it. Only a week earlier, turning up at the apartment and throwing himself down in the leather armchair, he'd kicked off with, "Well, where is she, where are you hiding her?"

Pretending ignorance, he'd replied, "Who do you mean? Who are you talking about?"

"Come on, there's no need to be coy. I only want to hear how you two've been getting on, that's all."

And so confessing the senora in question this far had kept her distance, he watched as an enraged Guzman began pacing about the room.

"Just who does that *rojo* bitch think she is after me going out of my way to put bread in her mouth? Let's take another little trip up to that dung-heap of a barrio of hers and then see how high and mighty she'll be."

"To tell you the truth, I'm not too greatly bothered. Desperate, even."

"Well, *she* certainly should be."

Guzman laughed.

127

"Speaking of which, how long is it since you've had a woman anyway, and not just in the kitchen either?"

After he'd gone on his way still chuckling, Furlong felt like throwing the window wide, for some of the Crab's malice seemed still to linger, polluting the apartment, associating him as he did now with something scuttling away leaving a trail of slime behind.

When dusk fell, the sky outside darkening to its usual inky hue, he brought out his bottle of Jameson's. Sitting there with the whiskey slowly loosening the knot inside, the years started falling away and he was back in a time and place once more recalling a certain other "someone" who'd also affected him in an unsettling way.

Her name was Bernadette and a redhead in a country with no scarcity of the type, although *she* seemed different somehow, smitten, as he was, by a painful case of unrequited calf-love. Miraculously, however, their paths managed to cross and they started going out together, meeting secretly on remote country roads or in woods or along river banks at nightfall, her parents, the problem, owning a chemist's shop and fierce chapel attenders while he was this farmer's son with dung on his boots and hands chapped from the daily milking round.

Nevertheless, the two young lovers pledged eternal, undying love, and when the call went out to put on the blue shirt and sail to Spain with the others, it seemed the ideal moment to receive everyone's blessing, and when he returned, a national hero, a place would be laid for him at the Kelly's big mahogany dinner-table, maybe even a position behind the counter of the family business as well.

However, after the letters from home became more and more infrequent, eventually ceasing altogether, he learned that Bernadette had been shipped off to an elderly aunt in Donegal, as near enough being sent to a convent as makes no difference, and after that he was never to hear of, or from her, again, Ireland being the hard unforgiving, old harridan of a country she was then.

Yet in spite of all of that, it looked as if he might be letting himself in for more of the same again, and at his age, too, for God's sake.

Waking the following morning, light flooding the apartment, the sounds from the street below also were pouring in, while drifting up came the unmistakeable aroma of freshly brewed coffee. A *carahillo*, a café *nero* with a slug of *conac*, would settle both head and stomach before going to ground with the door barred against anyone or anything from the world beyond.

El Retiro, as it was known, opened early for the workmen who'd then hang around outside hoping to be hired for the day, and when he entered, Paco Francisco, who rarely spoke or even glanced at his customers, set down a *vaso* of strong black coffee with its added shot of brandy in front of him.

On the bar lay a copy of that day's *Sur* with a photograph of some visiting big shots on its front page along with a bull-fighter in his suit of lights, and Furlong thought he recognised him from one of the posters pasted outside, even though all these boyish young heroes looked as though poured from the same mould, same tight-waisted monkey jacket, same skin-tight breeches, same pig-tailed, oiled black hair.

He'd only ever been to one *corrida,* which had been

specially laid on for them in Caceres when they first arrived here in Spain, and they, the Irish, had cheered on the bull instead of its human adversary. That combination of blood and sand had quickly palled, however, despite Guzman regularly coaxing him to join him in the presidential box along with the mayor and his good friend the police captain, and scanning the photograph in the newspaper, Furlong thought he recognised Delgado in the background, which was his cue to quickly drain his glass and head out into the already punishing glare of the street once more.

On the way to his apartment, stopping dead in his tracks, then drawing into the shade of a jacaranda tree, he felt his hangover return with a renewed ferocity. Luckily, however, *she* hadn't seen *him*, but he had spotted *her* outside Las Golondrinas peering at what looked like a piece of paper in her hand.

Hearing the familiar screech of the gate to his block followed by the rasping tones of the old busybody who seemed to permanently haunt its ground floor, emerging from his hiding-place, he saw the look of surprise on both the faces of the women standing there.

With a petulant "Senor Furlong", it was his neighbour who spoke out first, but before she'd time to launch into a tirade of complaint, his visitor repeated his name, and finding his own voice, in the best Spanish he could muster, he said, "My apologies for keeping you waiting, senora, but now that we're both here why don't we go inside and proceed with the business in hand?"

Leading the way up the stairs, trying not to draw attention to his limp, it suddenly struck him he still didn't know her name, although she, it seemed, knew his.

Reaching his apartment, after the door closed, both stood awkwardly inside as though waiting for the other to speak first, until, unbuttoning her coat and glancing around for somewhere to hang it, she waited for him to make the next move, so he gestured to one of the chairs at the table, and folding the *chaqueta* carefully and neatly she laid it over its back. Then she went into the kitchen and he heard the tap running followed by the soft clash of his dirty dishes being washed.

A little while later she came back carrying a broom, something he hadn't even realised he even possessed, and began brushing the floor with the same silent dedication he remembered his mother once employed. Next, she started dusting the furniture, and just as he was warming to the idea of leaving her to it, she accidentally knocked over a jar full of small change on the table, as after one of his late nights his pockets usually ended up weighed down with the stuff.

For an instant both stared in shock at the contents scattered on the floor, until dropping down, she began scooping them up, the shame of seeing her on her knees like that propelling him from his chair to kneel alongside her helping before she resumed her dusting.

When it came time for her to go into the bedroom, however, he was alarmed at the thought of the disarray she would find in there, but after what seemed like another very long interval she emerged and began putting on her outdoor coat while he sat wondering if this was how it would be, barely a word passing between them.

Finding his voice, he said, "We still haven't discussed the matter of payment yet."

"I'm perfectly happy to leave that up to you, senor," she

131

replied, with the merest hint of a smile. "But surely that can be settled next time I come here."

"Next time?"

"Si. Again for *you* to decide."

"When? Two? Three days? Four?"

Her smile was unmistakeable now.

"A week on Wednesday, if you still consider it necessary. Shall we say about the same time then?"

When the door closed, traces of her scent still lingered, something fresh, youthful, even, not heavy and cloying like the perfume most Spanish women her age preferred, and hoping to keep it trapped, he closed the window, staring down at the street, waiting to hear the gate opening then shutting below.

The glass muffled the sound, but he could still see her with her hand on the latch, then, moments later, standing on the empty street looking about her as though getting her bearings before walking away straight-backed in her long dark woollen coat.

His head had started throbbing, so he went into the bedroom to lie down, becoming instantly aware of what had taken place here, for the room had undergone a transformation, not just the bed made, but everything else returned to how it must have been before he first moved in. Even the air smelt different, more wholesome, more natural.

His clothes, too, including his underwear, which usually lay where he'd left them on the floor, had also been tidied away, and curious to see what she'd done with them he peered in the chest of drawers. Neatly folded and ordered, there they lay, a reminder of just how slovenly he'd become of late.

Turning his attention back to the bed, covers drawn tight as sailcloth, it seemed a sin to consider even stretching out on such taut perfection, so he began pulling out other drawers, feasting on the unexpected order there, until sorting through the layers of shirts he came on something stowed away, out of sight, as he thought, only now someone else might have recognised it for what it was.

Taking up the framed photograph of him and his old comrades of the Fifteenth, he cursed himself for not getting shot of it instead of leaving it to fester with the power to convict with evidence of a past he'd been trying to erase. There, too, were his discharge papers, the Bishop of Galway's medal, the Caceres postcard, the scorched missal salvaged from the bombed church in the same place, all wrapped in the pages of *The Cork Examiner* with its front-page picture of them about to board ship for Spain.

Delving down deeper, he uncovered something harder in outline, more worrying, also, and unwrapping its covering of khaki rag recognised the 30 mm Russian Nagant, recalling how it been taken from the dead hand of an International Brigader by one of the Moorish irregulars then bartered for an alarm clock, finally smuggled back home at the bottom of his own duffel bag. Why he'd held on to it, he'd no idea, never having drawn a bead on anyone, not even when he did see some front line action, and sitting there on the edge of the bed, that combination of cold metal and the scent of Vaseline soaked rag brought back other memories.

Like the rest of the brigade he'd heard of the Moorish irregulars' reputation, how when they entered a town they slaughtered everything before them, not only human, but dogs, cats, pigs, even, it was reported, cutting off the heads of the children's dolls in reprisal. While all this would be taking place, the Irish would be dug in further to the rear, until one time, having been ordered to advance, they were to experience that final mopping-up operation after the Moors had been sent in.

Somewhere in New Castile, it was, backward, agricultural, but according to intelligence a nest of rabid Reds and freemasons, and when they arrived they could see the captured prisoners already lined up in the main plaza with a scrap of something white pinned to their chests for the firing-squads to aim at. All those poor bastards still in their farm clothes, reminding him of country labourring types back home.

The nationalists of the town had come out of hiding and were dressed for the occasion, the men sporting hats and ties for the first time in months, and their wives, sweethearts, daughters in the most expensive of pre-war outfits.

Many of these former *ricos* were watching the shootings from their balconies as though expressly laid on for their entertainment, the women appearing to enjoy it even more than their menfolk, flourishing their fans and crying "Bravo!" and "Viva Franco!" after every volley. God forgive him, but he could feel his own blood race, and when the republican mayor and his party officials were dragged out to face the bullets he cheered along with rest of the Fifteenth.

The killings continued, bodies piling up where they fell, the air filled with the reek of cordite and stink of death, blood, shit, piss, until the last of the leftists' corpses were hauled away by the Moors in lorries. Except that Colonel Adolfo Ramirez, *jefe* of the operation, had a final treat to stir the loins of the senoras and senoritas of the town.

A group of women workers from the local canning factory, all *socialistas* and union members, were brought out and lined up while the crowd whistled and catcalled. Some already had their heads shaved to the bone making them look younger, like boys, in fact, giving rise to even more sexual insults from those above while he and the other Blueshirts stood in silence, the brandy curdling in their insides, even the hardest feeling uneasy at the sight of females treated in this fashion even if they were Reds.

What occurred next, however, was even more shocking, for as the firing-squad took aim, in a brazen gesture of contempt, raising their skirts above their heads, the women exposed themselves, before being cut down like a row of scythed wheat, and that image had stayed scorched on his brain until now, sitting here cradling a dead man's looted pistol in his hand.

After he'd wrapped it in its oily rag and stowed it in a safer place between the slats of the bed and the mattress, he must have drifted off, and when he awoke the dream he'd been having still lingered in his head, lower down, as well, aroused there as though the memory of those Spanish factory women had become confused with the person who'd been in his bedroom earlier.

All in all pretty pathetic, really, someone his age still behaving like that young fool he'd left behind in Leitrim yearning after a glimpse of red hair and a pale Burberry coat materialising out of the shadows by the river bank when he brought down the cows there to drink.

Lying back with closed eyes, he imagined he could still hear their lowing as they ambled ahead of him towards the house where the lamp in the kitchen window was lit and food waited on the table, an image untouched by anything that might surface later to spoil it, like that tiny hoard of keepsakes now hidden away once more under him.

DIEGO

Once, sweeping the floor of his father's barber's shop then taking the droppings out to be burned at the back, a task he hated as nothing smells as bad as singed hair, a commotion was heard outside, and so lathering and shaving were suspended until someone brought the news that Crazy Raoul, Senora Peralta's son, had escaped and was running naked like a very devil from hell in the street again, and crowding to the door, tracking him by the yelling, they were able to chart his progress to the Mount of the Madonna at the other end of the barrio. Then, as always, the question arose, would he be stopped in time before throwing himself down on the rocks there below?

However, as in so many of his other failed attempts, he was captured and brought back to his mother's house on Calle Rosario to be seen staring out gripping its window bars, something from their past he might have shared with Adriana when she came home from work. Except that lately any meal-time conversation between them had dried up, both immersed in their own thoughts while the radio burbled in the background.

Thinking back on all of that now, he realises he's been staring across at the house opposite, specifically at his neighbour's geranium in its pot behind the downstairs grille, that splash of crimson like a raw wound there against the white glare of the wall.

This morning the entire street's deathly still, only a solitary cat sunning itself on the doorstep of the house with the geranium, until returning to the window for yet another fruitless survey, he stiffens, having spotted the two Civil Guards now on the scene, drawing back, counting off the minutes until they've moved away.

But when he looks out again they're still there, a couple of surly looking brutes in dark green uniforms and glazed leather tricorn hats, one older, with a bushy moustache, the other skinny, almost a youth.

As he watches, the younger one strolls over to his neighbour's house, her cat scudding off as though even it senses danger, but before the cop has time to raise a fist to hammer on the door, it swings open, the old bitch herself appearing.

The young Guard has his back to him, but although he can't hear a word he can still read the woman's expression, not that of someone alarmed by the *policia* turning up on her doorstep, but someone at ease, and so he continues peering down imagining the worst. Which might be what exactly? That she's reporting suspicious sounds coming from an empty house across the street?

Finally, after the two have moved on, to calm himself down

he climbs up to where the current exercise-book lies open on the table as once the ink starts flowing the present gives way to the past, like in Madrid that time, when everyone was convinced the Republic was on the verge of victory and that Franco and his Africanistas would be driven back across the Straits.

As a visiting rural delegate of the UGT, he'd found the city a tremendous shock at first, the streets choked with people waving flags, yelling competing slogans of the Left, while the front itself was barely a score of kilometres away with their own side going out to engage with the enemy in the city's double-decker buses and taxis as though travelling to a picnic, then returning at night to eat and sleep with their families.

Then everything changed with the overhead whine of the German and Italian aircraft and their bombs, and with his brigade he marched towards Valencia, seeing the destruction as he went, crops burned, villages sacked by the Moorish *Regulares* who raped the women and grabbed the men by the shirt looking for the telltale bruise from a rifle's recoil on their right shoulder.

All along that ravaged route to the coast they passed columns of old men, women and children carrying bedding, furniture, even gramophones and sewing-machines on their backs, all trying to reach the sea and safe passage to France. But when they got to the port the British ships sent to rescue them had turned back, and people were throwing suitcases in the water, the sea turning yellow from the saffron inside, almost as valuable as gold, and searching for his own account of that particular episode he began pulling down the exercise-books from the shelf in front of him.

*

At some point he heard the church bell strike three which meant he'd been sitting ankle-deep in scattered paper all this time, nothing passing his lips since early morning, and so padding down to where Adriana had laid out a bowl of gazpacho along with some of yesterday's bread, he tried to eat.

On the kitchen wall was a cheap oleograph of the Virgin clasping the infant Jesus to her breast, and even though he made a point of turning his face away he still imagined that long-suffering stare drilling into the small of his back, Adriana insisting on it hanging there as evidence of religious adherence in case anyone ever gained entrance to the house.

So far he hadn't drunk any of the wine in the carafe he'd taken down from the cupboard, but now he poured himself a glass, then helped himself to another just as he'd done on that night when he and Adriana had words because of it and she'd turned her back on him and went to sleep. Or pretended to, over on her own side of that invisible barrier between them like those unhappy couples who resorted to a dividing bolster down the middle of the bed.

For some reason the level in the carafe appeared to have fallen quite dramatically, and staring at it he tried to work out just how many glasses he'd had even though the evidence of his head seemed pretty incontrovertible, and so if he already wasn't drunk he wasn't far off. Still, even though his legs weren't functioning as well as they might, his brain felt fine, and rising from the table he climbed once more to his cramped retreat at the top of the house determined on taking care of something he should have attended to a long time ago.

Worryingly, up there the floor now seemed littered with his

exercise-books as though a stranger had broken in and laid waste in his absence, so in his head he's hearing the sound of heavy boots on the stairs and voices calling out that the *rojo's* secret hiding place has finally been uncovered. However, before any of that can come about he must dispose of the evidence just like Adriana did with the family photographs that time, and going down on his hands and knees he begins scooping up the scattered blue-backed hoard.

But then what? Certainly not their burning, for even if they fed the stove one volume at a time at night the smell would only create suspicion. So what if Adriana smuggled out the offending material herself, throwing it down a disused well where so many other incriminating human remains had ended up, until the thought struck him how could he even propose something as charged as that if they still couldn't conduct a normal conversation over their evening meal together.

Staring at the longest penned confession of guilt in the history of the pueblo on the floor in front of him, it was as if something else had become crystal clear as well, for it wasn't just when they were eating or were in bed together that something had changed. *She* had, remembering, as he did, how she used to talk freely about the hotel and the people there, but now didn't, and never having given much thought of her in the company of strangers before, other men, suddenly he was seeing her through *their* eyes, someone still with the same dark-eyed looks which had first captivated him.

It had been there in the likeness taken in a photographer's studio in Malaga in the early days of their courtship, she with a posy in her hand, he holding a straw fedora, the only occasion he'd allowed himself be seen wearing such a bourgeois object.

The photograph had been one of those removed from their frames and burned, and he could still recall how their younger faces, frozen by the camera's lens, curled up then turned to ash in front of them, and now history seemed to be repeating itself, and sitting there he heard a noise below, making him think of the two Guards earlier.

But the dreaded tattoo of knuckles on wood didn't arrive. Instead, the creak of the front door opening, followed by a familar soft footfall, although why was she returning at this early hour?

Finally, the smell of cooking drove him below where the now near empty carafe still sat on the table, and when he sat down to eat, going to the cupboard, she took down a fresh one, setting it in front of him without a word, and so the slow purgatory of yet another fraught evening began.

When the meal finished, he stared at the wine in the carafe, same ruby red as the Sacred Heart on the wall behind him, and he was still blearily considering the significance of this when Adriana murmured a grudging good night, heading straight off up to bed.

After she'd gone, unable to bear the silence any longer, drawing up his chair to the radio he waited for the valves to heat, then that first crackle of static make itself heard. When a speaker's voice did emerge, male, hectoring, he twisted the knob until he found some classical music, always a safer option. Sitting in the near dark, the only light coming from the dial of the radio, reaching for the carafe, he poured the first of what was to become even more glasses on top of those he'd already had, so that next thing he knew he was slumped forward, cheek resting on the beached, scrubbed wood of the table.

He must have been asleep some considerable time, for when he awoke it was as though a shroud had descended out there, enveloping the entire barrio in the same deadening slumber. Yet something had alerted him, this low, dimmed cacophony, swelling, until it seemed to be coming up the street towards him. A jingling of cow-bells, sly giggling laughter, telling him it was the *cerrancia* when people took to the streets after dark to mock those who'd broken the conventions of the pueblo, usually sexual.

Listening intently, to his horror it sounded as though the shuffling throng had come to a halt outside his own front door, although why should they wish to single out someone who didn't exist, a ghost?

Straining hard, he tried to catch a whispered mention of his own name but detected nothing recognisable, until finally someone struck a cow bell, the rest banging what he took to be kitchen pots and pans, and his tormentors moved off, trailing on up the street taking their small-minded petty spite and rancour with them somewhere else.

A finger of wine was left in the carafe, so he poured and drank it after what seemed like a narrow escape. Yet the danger had come and gone, so his secret existence was still safe, until the worrying thought crept into his head that *he* mightn't have been the one in the *cerrancia's* sights after all, for what if the people out there knew something about Adriana and her life down on the costa he didn't? Even more terrifying, what if that brief stop of theirs outside was a rehearsal for the real thing?

ADRIANA

Although it's been three weeks now she's been coming to *Las Golondrinas,* the woman there still glares at her when she enters the block, and climbing the stairs and entering the *irlandes'* apartment she hangs her coat on the hook she suspects he's had placed there for that express purpose, after which she begins her duties while he sits reading his daily *Sur*.

This day, while she's in the kitchen, he comes in and opens one of the cupboards and she sees it's crammed with all manner of foodstuffs, ham, eggs, cheese, beans, bread, and even though she's never looked into this foreigner's larder before she senses it might only have been recently stocked in this way.

For a moment they both stand staring at the embarrassment of riches, making her wonder if it's there to impress her with a glimpse of a world where there are those who eat better than most and those like herself who don't, until realising what's really behind it, she enquires, "Would you like for me to cook for you as well, senor?"

And just as formally, he replies, "Only if it's convenient and not any kind of an imposition."

However, she's perfectly at ease with the suggestion as her normal duties can be completed in an hour, two at the most, and so she begins preparing something simple, a frittata with eggs, an onion, tomatoes, a pepper.

Rummaging in the *irlandes'* kitchen cupboards in search of a frying pan feels a little like looking through his bedroom chest of drawers on her first day here. Although what she uncovered then left her determined to forget what she'd seen under the socks and underwear, leading her to think of Diego and his reaction if he were to find out she'd prepared a meal for someone whose past was still a threat and possibly a present danger as well.

After she finished the dish, bringing it into him in the living-room and setting it down on the little round table there, the *irlandes* stared at the plate in front of him.

"Is it not to your satisfaction, senor?"

"Oh, not at all. It's much better than I could hope to deserve."

Taking it as a compliment, preparing to leave, she reaches for her coat on its hook on the wall, but pointing to a chest in the corner, he says, "There's some wine in there. Glasses, as well."

While she's opening the *tinto,* he says, "Why not make that two glasses instead of one?"

After she's set the bottle down on the table along with just the one glass, looking up from his plate, he says, "You're

145

certain now you won't join me? It' just that I don't much care to drink on my own if I don't have to."

"Gracias, but no, senor," she tells him, followed by the lie, "There's someone waiting for me at home," except that it's not really an untruth after all.

"Well, never mind, perhaps you'll do me the honour next time."

Bidding him *buenas tardes* and closing the door behind her she goes down to where the woman below is patiently waiting to track her departure with that same resentful, beady-eyed stare of hers.

Outside, walking away, she hears a voice call out behind her, "Senora! Senora!" followed by an insistent, more troubling cry of, "Dona Adriana!" and turning she sees it's that brash young waiter Pepe from the Miramar.

"Such a pleasure to see you again, Dona Adriana. But, forgive me for asking, have you managed to find some other employment yet?"

"Not really at the moment ... But how are things with *you*?"

Shrugging, he looks up at the sky.

"Life goes on, you know how it is."

"And the hotel?"

"The guests come, they go, while we remain the same."

"And Carlotta?"

"She, also."

Glancing over his shoulder, he says, "To tell you the truth, you left at the right time. Don Gustavo now works us twice as hard as before. There's talk of a new hotel getting built. More beds, more guests, more competition."

"All the same, let's trust life will be kind to you."

"And to you, also, Dona Adriana. You, also ..."

After he's strolled away with a backward wave of the hand, she lingers for a moment surprised at how easily she'd handled their conversation. Even so, she still worries he might have seen her coming out of *Las Golondrinas*. But then he's young, she tells herself, and so not much given to putting two and two together.

Taking one of the narrow streets leading down to the sea, reaching the *playa* there, she slips off her shoes, the shingle along the water's edge slowing her to a barefoot trudge towards the headland, where, turning inland, she'll continue on her way through the cane fields back to the barrio. Usually this stretch of beach is one she has all to herself, but today she can make out a thin column of smoke rising ahead, and curious to see where it's coming from she wades in the shallows right up to the promentory itself.

Scrambling up to the summit and gazing down the other side she sees this little group of intruders below, her nose picking up the scent of fish cooking over a driftwood fire.

These youthful strangers with their blond hair look like foreigners, one of them a girl, and coming back from her work in the dark she remembers seeing other fires like this one, hearing, too, the voices and the music from their radios of other young *americanos* so at ease in her own country yet so far from their own.

As she watches, something seems to have set off a flurry of alarm below there, and following the direction of their gaze, she spots its cause, the two mounted civil guards on the crest of the dunes high above looking down, the young people backing away now right to the water's edge. And suddenly it's like a scene from one of those silent films she and Diego would watch in the square with the rest of the village when the travelling cinema came to the barrio, the ranch-owner's hired hands riding down the fleeing homesteaders, except that these two home-grown black hats, sitting back in their saddles, have stopped to share a cigarette, enjoying the sight of their shivering victims up to their waists out there in the sea.

However, knowing how this particular episode turns out, there's no need to watch any further, and so lowering herself down on to the sand on the other side of the headland she sets off on her way back home through the cane fields.

After the freshness of the breeze from the sea the air here feels heavy and smothering, so that by the time she reaches the outskirts of the barrio she's eager to drink from the water-spouts at the church then bathe her face and arms in that chill rush piped down from the sierras. Up there the peaks are still capped in white, even though she has never seen snow falling herself. Diego, however, has, when fighting in the North, and although looking picturesque on a Christmas card it can quickly turn the soles of your boots to damp felt then blotting-paper. That's what he told her, anyway.

Nearer home and about to turn into Calle Agua, she sees one of the barrio's many donkeys coming towards her, and recognising the figure on its back she draws into an alleyway waiting for both to pass. But coming to a halt in the middle of the narrow street the beast looses a cascade of dung on the cobbles, and spotting her there, the *burro's* owner calls out to her.

"What brings you back here, Dona Adriana, after enjoying the life down on the costa with all the rich *extranjeros* there? Tell me, is it true..?"

Pausing, his old peasant eyes moisten at the thought of all that only dreamed-of excess, until, shaking its harness, the donkey kicks out, braying, and they amble on off up the street together.

After the patter of hooves fades off in the distance the splashing of water in the trough outside the church sounds even more tempting, but dreading coming on some of the women washing their clothes there she moves quickly on to her own house, and once inside stands breathing in the familiar smells of the kitchen before going to the water-jar on the table and drinking long and deep.

Filling a basin, she then washes her hands and face, but feeling hot and clammy still she peels everything off right down to the thin cotton *camisola* next her skin. Sensing something, some *one*, turning, she sees Diego standing at the foot of the stairs watching her, and ashamed at being observed like this, she covers herself, and he climbs back up to his retreat as though having seen something different about her, something she's brought back with her from that other new life of hers.

In the cupboard there's a couple of eggs and an end piece of ham, enough to put a meal for them together, and soon the smell of hot oil and garlic is filling the kitchen, sufficient to coax Diego down from his lair. However, after both plates have been placed on the table, he still hasn't appeared, so she sits down herself and starts eating without him, and when she's finished she washes her own dish in the sink.

Yet still no sound from above, no soft slither of slippers on

149

the stairs, and so a slow anger starts mounting inside at the thought of him treating her and the meal she's cooked for him in this way, and taking up the untouched plate on the table she empties the contents into the slop bucket and standing there feels the tears flow.

It's been a long time since she's given in to her emotions in this way, and with the music from the radio muffling her sobs she's thinking of all those other women whose grief has also had to stay locked away inside, just as in that same way only the drunkard or the mad are ever to be heard laughing in the street in this doomed country of hers.

EUGENE

Travelling to Malaga by bus took nearly an hour and a half and so when he finally arrived the shops had all brought down their shutters for the siesta. At four they would roll back up again so he'd time on his hands to sit in the shade of the tree-lined Alameda watching the locals pass by.

Sitting there in his creased summer suit and with his ruddy Northern complexion, he soon became a target for beggars, many propelling themselves on wheeled boards or shuffling along crab-like on stumps.

However, he must have dozed off, for when he awoke a gypsy woman was sitting alongside him smiling companionably as though they were resting before moving on together. He could detect a pungent reek of wood-smoke from her clothes along with something more rank, and getting up to walk away, expecting a volley of abuse, which didn't arrive, he realised she was blind, and he dropped a couple of centimos in her lap, hearing her utter something halfway between a murmur and a moan, her face uplifted in that strange, unsettling, trusting way all sightless people seem to present to the world.

There was a bar near the city's cathedral he knew, and moving out from the shelter of the giant tropical trees lining the Alameda and crossing Calle Martinez where the sun pounced like some fiery ravening beast, he sat down in the cool calm of the garden at the front of the place and ordered a beer.

Because of the cathedral close by a few shifty looking individuals could be seen peddling religious items on its steps until a pair of civil guards strolled up and instantly they'd melt away with their postcards and cheap trinkets, medals, usually, just like the one in his possession at this moment. Feeling pleasantly reflective because of that first San Miguel *grande* and a second one on the way, he took out the little burnished disc, turning it over in his palm, thinking of the one whose name was inscribed on its face and as also so happened was the reason he'd travelled to the city today.

After the sleepy tempo of the resort he'd just come from the din and bustle of this great seaport seemed to be that of some other country, and when the bells overhead struck the afternoon middle hour, they, too, sounded foreign, and soon he heard the shops opening their doors which was his cue to go in search of the little Lebanese tailor near the Plaza de Felix Saenz.

The last time he'd visited his establishment had been close to a score or so years earlier. Reassuringly, it seemed as if nothing had really changed, same gloomy, grimy exterior, and inside, the same rows of wardrobes on either side of that one full-length, mottled mirror. And Melek, too, although more stooped, wearing the same English top-coat despite the heat, a tape measure looped about its velvet collar, as effusively welcoming as ever. As he liked to boast, he never forgot a face, just as he prided himself on remembering a client's measurements, those restless, black button eyes of his seeming to anticipate a customer's wants before even uttering a word.

Head to one side, the little tailor smiled encouragingly.

"Something perhaps a little less workaday this time, senor? A *pocito* more *formal*, shall we say?"

Catching sight of his own startled face in the mirror, Furlong wondered if the entire world could now see him for what he was, naked and exposed even before stripping to his underwear for a first fitting. Not that he was in the market for anything bespoke this time.

"Very well," sighed Melek, "if the senor's set on something ready-made I may just have something that might fit his particular frame."

Drawing apart the doors of one of the cavernous wardrobes he unhooked a garment hanging inside.

"Come, try this on," he ordered, shaking out the jacket like it was a matador's cape, and, indeed, it did have a particular sheen to it, the weave catching the light in some almost theatrical way.

"Dove grey barathea with an Italian silk and alpaca blend. Sadly, the senor, a senator, passed away before he could get around to wearing it."

Slipping his arms into the lining of the sleeves, they did indeed feel chillier to the touch than was normal. Still, this was no time to be squeamish about a dead man's property.

"Does it feel comfortable? No restrictions anywhere?"

"No, no, it's fine. But what about the rest?"

"Ah, *los pantalones.* The senator ordered two pairs."

Standing there, bare-legged, experiencing the air about his extremities made him feel even more vulnerable than he already was, so he said, "One pair I'm sure will be enough."

"In that case, try these on," said the little tailor, discreetly turning away while Furlong hopped into the *pantalones,* the expression always sounding effeminate to his ears, more so, right now, caught literally with his pants down and in a pair too long in the leg although the waist felt about right.

"Could I have these be altered if I came back later?"

"In one hour's time your purchases will be waiting for you."

Uncoiling the tape measure from about his neck, then quickly running it down both seams, Melek murmured something in his own language while Furlong climbed back into his old linen trousers again which seemed somehow much baggier now, clown-like, almost.

At seven o'clock when the city's clerks and business types were purposefully criss-crossing the plaza after work he made his way back to Melek who had his two-piece ready for him. After trying it on he handed over what seemed like an excessive amount for something needing only minor alterations, Melek insisting on a parting glass of his homeland's local firewater which Furlong drank down in one, scalding his gullet.

"Senor, in my country we have a saying, fine clothes open all doors, and often certain hearts as well."

He was smiling as he said it, making Furlong feel as though he was standing in his underwear all over again, and leaving the shop, still smarting, he stopped at the bar at the bus-station where he ordered a *conac,* then several more, so missing his last bus home along the coast.

In the taxi taking him there he must have fallen asleep, only coming to hearing the driver call out he'd left his *paquete* in the back seat. Then there was another blank interval before finding himself in his apartment sitting staring at the invisible sea murmuring somewhere out there in the darkness.

On the table squatted the indistinct shape of something he seemed to have recently acquired but couldn't work out how or why, the contents remaining equally mysterious.

The following morning, waking stiff and aching in the arm-chair, he could hear the church bells ringing, telling him it was a Sunday, and after relieving himself in the bathroom he went back to the living-room to examine what lay on the table.

One thing became immediately apparent, whoever had wrapped it in stiff, buff-coloured paper then criss-crossed it with twine took obvious pride in their handiwork, the knots doubled, then retied, and getting a kitchen knife he sliced through the cord, carefully lifting out the soft weight of heady-smelling fabric inside.

The jacket he draped over a chair, leaving the trousers flat, still folded on the table, both items still looking like someone else's property, not some rough and ready Celt badly needing a shave.

Still, perhaps he was being over-hasty, and putting on the suit and going into the bedroom where the wardrobe had a long narrow mirror he was confronted by this nattily-dressed stranger staring back at him, only the face and hands spoiling the effect.

Never had he possessed something so stylish or well-cut as this, smelling also of the old-fashioned lavender his mother scented the linings of drawers with back home. Luxuriating in the sensation, he began strolling about the apartment wondering what the neighbours might make of this dapper stranger, until tiring of such foolishness he hung the dead senator's two-piece in the wardrobe along with all those other secrets hidden away there in that room.

Next day he mooched about the apartment, finally taking up an old paperback, a Western with redskins on the cover. Then, becoming bored with the plot, he went back to pacing back and forth, finally staring down at the street outside longing for a certain figure to appear, until as the day slid towards late afternoon he realised he must have got the day wrong.

However, when the moment *did* arrive two mornings later he was unprepared with lathered cheeks and razor in his hand. For an instant they both stood there, not speaking, as though strangers, and after she came inside, hanging up her coat on the hook as usual, the same uneasy, awkward atmosphere prevailed, she intent on her dusting and cleaning and he in his armchair pretending to be deep in his Wild West novel.

Some time later when she went into the bedroom he found himself listening out for the creak of the wardrobe door, imagining the look on her face when she saw the latest addition hanging inside, and just as he was wondering if she might offer to cook for him again, perhaps even join him this time, the world outside came crashing in.

There was the sound of a heavy-footed ascent on the stairs,

an equally brutal tattoo on the door, then an all too recognisable voice calling out, "Come on, amigo, I know you're in there! Don't worry, I promise to be a fly on the wall, seeing nothing, hearing nothing!"

Despite it being early still, his unwelcome visitor already sounded drunk, and even though he decided to wait for him to tire and go back the way he came, he wavered, buckling when the other's tone became more threatening.

"Have a care, amigo, it's not wise insulting old friends in this cosy little *costa* corner of ours."

Opening the door he was confronted by a grinning Guzman with what looked like a bottle of whiskey held in his hand.

"This, I have to tell you," he announced, brandishing the bottle, "wasn't easy to get hold of after you and your Americano friend practically drank the Miramar dry of the stuff. But, while on the subject of aquaintances, how's your other *amiga* these days? I trust she's been proving accommodating."

Inside the apartment now, he'd commandeered the armchair, Furlong suddenly aware of Adriana's coat hanging on its hook by the door.

"Well, are we going to break open this offering of mine, or are we not?"

Going into the kitchen, and returning with a couple of tumblers and a jug of water, Furlong hoped might provide a distraction, but after he'd poured them measures apiece Guzman stared accusingly at the glass in Furlong's hand.

"My choice of firewater not to your taste? Or perhaps you've no wish to drink with an old friend?"

157

"What do you mean?"

"Well, look at what you've given yourself. Barely enough to wet the bottom of the glass."

"To tell the truth, I've been laying off it a bit of late."

"As some of your other good friends in the Hollywood Room have noticed, even thinking you'd turned your back on them. Until I informed them, that is, it might be down to a romantic priority elsewhere."

His concern must have shown on his face, for Guzman gave a loud laugh.

"No need to look quite so alarmed, amigo, your secret's perfectly safe with me. Incidentally, just how *are* you and the *rojo's* widow getting on? Don't tell me you haven't bedded her yet. During the war, you may recall, we introduced a fair number of the ladies of the Left to the old rub-a-dub-dub. You might even have taken part in some of the fun yourself."

Sitting having to listen to this filth, Furlong wondered how much more of it he could take from this son of a bitch now reaching his glass forward for a refill, and pointedly ignoring the request, he saw the other's face darken.

"So that's how the land lies now, is it? In bed with the enemy in more ways than one, are we? Still, I wonder does the same enemy know you and I were on the same side that bumped off that late husband of hers? Or is that no longer of significance? That *rojo* bitch may have blinded *you, irlandes*, but not Luis Casares Guzman here, nor Captain Enrique Delgado either. He and I and those like us who gave our all for our beloved Espana will never forget nor forgive those who once were its enemy."

"Well, forgive me if I don't care to take advice on something like that from someone who never actually set foot on a battlefield himself. Mind you, that's only what I've heard people say behind your back. Still, I imagine there's more than a grain of truth in it."

It may have been the whiskey talking, but he no longer cared, the person on the receiving end staring at him now with venom in his eyes.

"One of these nights, asleep in your bed, amigo, and that republican whore slips a knife between your ribs, you'll remember my words. But if she still hasn't moved in with you yet, advise her to get a move on before that house of hers is appropriated and handed over to someone more loyal to the state."

After he'd gone the other's words seemed to leave a residue behind like the slime his namesake might deposit before creeping off to hide under a rock somewhere, Furlong regretting not getting in a parting shot of his own, even letting the bastard have it over the head with the bottle he brought. However, needing all the courage he could muster to face the one on the other side of the wall, he steeled himself.

Head bowed, she was sitting on the edge of bed when he opened the door and looked in.

"Listen, all that stuff you might have overheard in there, sure, it was nothing more than a lot of ' drunken talk. None of it means a thing, pay no attention to it."

However, clearly she had, for there were tears in her eyes, and rising from the bed and smoothing the covers as though erasing any impression she might have left there, she moved past him into the living-room, reaching up to take her coat down from its hook on the wall.

"Senor, my work is finished here," she said, and thinking she meant for good, he said, "But not before I give you something," holding out the little silver religious medal with her name on it. Taking it from him, she stared at it.

"Again let me apologise, for I never should have allowed that man who was here speak of you in that way. He was in the wrong and so was I. But, please, please, don't just stand there, sit."

Hesitating for a moment, she lowered herself into the leather armchair, modestly covering her dark, stocking-clad knees, while he pulled forward one of the apartment's straight-backed chairs for himself.

"Senor . . ." she began.

"Call me Eugene, please. He might have been a pope or a saint or something, which is where the resemblance ends, of course. But then, I suppose, you already gathered that."

" Senor Eugenio, my *medalla,* did you find it here in your apartment?"

"No, but someone else did, and elsewhere. You might even have come across him when you were working in the hotel. They call him the Americano."

As soon as he said the name he realised he'd touched a raw nerve. But then why should she be put out learning that Johnnie was the finder and not him? There seemed no reason he could think of. Even so, resolving to take advantage of his big moment as he now saw it, he decided to confess, to come clean.

"Senora, twenty years or so ago, myself and a crowd of other

Irish Blueshirts, as we were known, came to your country to fight those wearing a uniform of a different colour, and in that short, dirty little war then I saw some terrible things, many still capable of giving me bad dreams. But even if you may have already managed to figure out some of that history for yourself, I'd hate you to think I was the same as that man who was in this room earlier."

After she'd heard him out, she stared at him.

"Senor Eugenio, I *know* you're not like that person, for one more of the same would be still one too many."

"Like Captain Delgado, you mean?"

"Si, and why it's best that I no longer come here."

"Do you think I *care* what those two, those two ... *cabron*, might, or might not do? Do you?"

Unthinking, he'd raised his voice, and seeing her glance at the bottle on the table, quickly he said, "No, no, I'm not drunk. Which is why, which is ..." leaving the rest hanging unsaid.

"But what about *you?* Losing your home? Maybe ending up on the street? Have you thought about *that?*"

Any fool, however, could see that she had, and continuing to press, he urged, "Why not make this present arrangement a permanent one and let Senor Guzman and his friends go to hell where they belong? And, anyway, why go back to an empty house? Stay here and eat with me instead. I mean, just think of all that food in there going to waste."

But already she'd risen to her feet, intending to pick up her bag which lay by the door, and for a crazy moment he thought of offering to fill it with some of those same provisions, until producing his wallet instead, he said, "Allow me, at least, to give you what I must owe you."

161

"You've already taken care of that, and more than generously."

"Even so, I'd like to contribute something extra. I mean, look at all the changes you've wrought here."

"There are plenty of others more than capable of providing the same service."

"But none like yourself, which is why this doesn't need to be the last time we meet, does it? Socially, perhaps? In the pueblo? In Calle El Capitano?"

The instant the words left his lips he realised all his hard-won gains had been squandered.

"You know where I *live*? You've *been* there?"

"No, no, not at all," he lied. "Although given an invitation, I feel sure I could find my way there."

"Senor, *your* place is here on the costa, while mine is with all those other poor people up in the barrio like me, and so you and I must carry on with our lives as we did before."

"Before? After you heard what Guzman said?"

"Si, senor, for there is no way you nor I can ever change that."

After the door closed behind her he stood there trying to make sense of what had just taken place, for why turn her back on what he'd offered if the alternative meant almost certain destitution? And why return to a lonely, empty house? Why? What for? But then perhaps the answer lay, not in *what*, but *who*, recalling something she'd said the first time she'd been here about someone waiting for her back there.

So now instead of feeling confused, he was angry, but not at himself for his own foolishness, but at *her* for keeping the

162

truth from him, for a moment even considering going after her before she vanished for good taking his dreams with her, just as another once did on a path by a river bank when he was younger and almost as green as the grass there himself.

JOHNNIE

The week before he was due to fly to Madrid for the *Noche de Estrelas* concert something told him a surprise send-off might be planned for him here in the hotel, and he felt genuinely touched having gotten fond of certain people in the place, principally young Jorge in the Hollywood Room when late at night they had the bar all to themselves.

Of course, when it came to confessional exchanges in the wee small hours Sinatra ruled the musical roost and so he had to hand it to his rival, raising a glass to his portrait on the back wall, Jorge innocently enquiring if he'd ever actually met The Voice.

"You could say our paths crossed on various occasions," he told him, and thankfully Jorge let the subject lie there without any unnecessary uncovering of old sores.

Even so, he still couldn't help teasing the kid.

"You do realise, don't you, this might be the last time you

and I get to shoot the breeze here like this. You *do* know I'm going to Madrid," the kid's face going pale.

"But *when,* Senor Johnnie?"

"I mean, does it matter?"

Again the same anguished look and even though he knew he shouldn't he was starting to get a kick out of mildly torturing the poor kid.

"Come on, you can spill the beans, I promise I won't tell a soul."

"But that would still only spoil the *surprisa,* senor."

Which is when he let the kid off the hook.

"*Una mas*, Senor Johnnie?"

"No, I guess I'm sorta okay with this one right now."

Clean living, of course, just for the sake of it wasn't the only reason he was nursing a couple of highballs a night instead of the customary half dozen, committed as he was now on staying intent on something other than his health. Or rather, *someone,* hoping that Furlong might show up and come clean, even though any fool could see the poor sap was in over his head with this Adriana dame.

Yet he still couldn't leave it alone, enquiring, "That woman you told me about when we were in Howie's, remember? You know, the one who lost her job here in the hotel."

"Senora Adriana, you mean?"

"So that's her name. It's just she might have left something of hers back in my room last time she was up there."

"And you wish to return it?"

"Yeah, but the thing is I don't know how or where to get in touch with her."

The kid stared down at the counter top he was polishing.

165

Then, naming a village some way off, he said, "One of the dining-room waiters, Pepe, comes from there. I could ask him to talk with you if you like."

"Pepe? Short, dark, kinda cocky?"

"Cocky, senor?"

"Yeah, *chulo*. Knows it all, to use an expression."

"Or imagines he does, Senor Johnnie?"

Both laughed.

"See, just look how much I've taught you in the short time I've been here, Jorge."

"Except now you are leaving us, Senor Johnnie."

True, but not before tying up one last little loose end, he's thinking to himself, watching the ice slowly dilute the vodka and soda in his glass.

The following day, a Sunday, surfacing early, for he really *was* living the boy scout life now, he saw Pepe was already waiting for him in reception, a grin lighting up his eager young face.

"Buenas dias, senor, everything has been arranged for you with your driver waiting outside."

"Driver?"

"Si, for our trip to my pueblo. When Jorge told me you wished to see something of our beautiful Andalusian countryside, Don Gustavo gave me permission to be your guide for the entire day."

"And did Jorge happen to say anything else?"

"Senor?"

"I mean, why *your* village in particular."

From the bemused look on the youngster's face, however, it would appear Jorge had been his usual discreet and tactful self.

166

Even so, already Johnnie was feeling like some kind of a fraud, for just what did he expect to discover when he got to this pueblo place anyway? He was also experiencing the familiar need for that first drink of the day, and when he saw his mode of transport outside he felt like heading back to the bar. Parked on the hotel's forecourt stood a smallish, cream-coloured limo, while the driver was wearing what looked like a chauffeur's peaked cap, for Christ's sake.

Climbing aboard, the curtained windows and heavy dark upholstery inside reminded him of a hearse, smelt like one, too, and sinking into all of that dusty moquette he resigned himself to going along for the ride. Staring straight ahead, dark peasant paws gripping the wheel, the driver still hadn't uttered a word. But then that same dumb stoniness was something he'd noted in a lot of the older people here who'd been through the tough years after Franco came to power.

Well on their way by now, their car was snaking around a succession of even more and more dizzying bends, while down to his left there was this terrifying drop to the fields below scarcely bigger than garden plots back home, their ordered rows of olive trees casting identical shadows on the parched looking soil.

Breaking the silence, he asked, "Is this the only route up from the coast?"

"Si, senor, but most people take to the *campo*."

"What about a bus?"

"Si, but only one a day and to Malaga."

The kid must have been wondering why he was asking all this stuff, but he was thinking of the woman day after day making her way down through those same fields to the hotel when she'd been employed there.

Finally, pointing on ahead, Pepe announced, "See, senor, my pueblo," and as the car rounded yet another bend, above them, clinging to the hillside like so many carelessly strewn sugar cubes, a cluster of dwellings came into view, one of the famous "white villages" Johnnie had read about.

Driving closer, they could hear the clanging of bells, and Pepe said, "While you're here you must visit our church, Senor Johnnie. People come from far away just to see the religious paintings inside."

"Why not, maybe later. Right now I'd like to get out and stretch my legs."

"But don't you wish to drive up into the pueblo, senor?"

Clearly Pepe's heart was set on some form of grand rolling entrance basking in the reflected glory of his famous Americano amigo, but putting on his sun glasses Johnnie was already stepping out into the fierce mid-day glare, and even though it was obvious he didn't speak any English the driver seemed to have got the message, pulling over to the side of the road and switching off the engine.

"The sun is *mucho fuerte*, Senor Johnnie. You should extra take care when not used to it."

"Where I come from it's also hot as hell this time of year. Didn't anyone ever tell you that?"

"No, Senor Johnnie."

Feeling sorry for the kid, Johnnie told him, "Tell you what, first bar we come to, we'll have a *copa* together, and afterwards you can give me the full guided tour, church, pictures, the works, okay?"

Thinking it might draw less attention to himself he'd left his expensive looking jacket in the car but within seconds his shirt was clinging to his back. Up here the air felt pre-heated as though in an oven, and already he was squinting ahead for signs of human habitation, even that bar he'd promised Pepe.

Still, there were signs tourists had been making inroads for he could see a couple of places with tables outside, and getting closer, shops selling the usual souvenir trash, sombreros, straw donkeys, hanging clusters of maracas and castanets.

Some of the locals were also starting to surface now, staring dead-eyed at them from doorways following their progress up what appeared to be the only paved street, and beginning to feel all this silent scrutiny getting to him, he suggested, "How about that one there?" pointing to a bar with a badly bellied awning while still promising some sort of shade.

"But there's one a little further on, Senor Johnnie, where a better class of person drinks."

"Like you and me, you mean?"

And even though he still had hopes of showing him off, the kid laughed.

"No, senor, for I am only this poor *pueblito* while you are this *persona mucho famosa*."

His insides were crying out now for that first measured gush of San Miguel, and he held out a couple of big peseta notes which Pepe immediately ignored, meaning he'd insulted him, although hopefully not for too long before he got round to his true motive in coming to this backward neck of the woods where the air hung heavy with the reek of wood-smoke and burro dung liberally carpeted the streets.

After the kid had gone in to get them both beers apiece he

dropped into one of the cane chairs outside the *Bar Deportivo*, while across the way a trio of barefoot urchins stood gaping at him, and when Pepe emerged with two glasses and the customary saucers of tapas he could almost sense their saliva glands going into overdrive.

But before he'd a chance to dip into his pocket for some change Pepe barked something at them and they went sloping off.

"I, too, was once like one of those young *chicos*, Senor Johnnie, but soon I will have saved up enough for a motor scooter, an Italian Vespa, the very first in the barrio."

"Well, bully for you, kiddo."

Then, determined on getting back down to business, he enquired, "When you come back home, ever run across that senora from here who used to take care of the bedrooms in the Miramar?"

For the briefest of moments the young face opposite went rigid.

"You mean Senora Adriana?"

"Yeah, if that's her name. I never really got a chance to thank her for the terrific job she always did."

"But we all do our best for the guests at the hotel."

"I know, which is why I never understood why she had to leave the way she did. I mean, do you know the reason?"

He could sense the kid was perturbed about where the conversation might be leading, and what happened next seemed to compound that uneasiness, when ambling into sight came a couple of civil guards in those dark green uniforms and comic opera hats of theirs, Pepe lowering himself down deeper in his chair.

170

The cops had spotted them and were slowing until near enough to give them that obligatory evil eye they all love to cultivate, one younger, tall, skinny, his older sidekick with a paunch and a heavy drooping moustache.

Right up to the bar they strolled, and still giving them the once-over, went inside.

"Another beer?"

But the kid shook his head.

"Okay, let's move on, then."

Keeping close to the houses on the shady side of the street, he saw that the three barefoot youngsters who'd earlier been checking him out were trailing them now, but not in any kind of sinister way, rather drifting listlessly along, the air in between the close-packed dwellings hanging heavy as though trapped like the people living here.

Soon, however, he heard the sound of water gushing from a pipe, or pipes, as it turned out, having reached the church where a stone trough was fed by a fast-flowing rush from the jaws of a row of carved lions' heads. After they'd both drunk from cupped hands, Pepe boasted, "Here we have the best *agua* in Spain, Senor Johnnie, straight from the sierras and never been known to stop flowing . . . But, come, let me show you the famous altar and the religious pictures inside."

Much smaller than expected, the interior was a bare, simple place of worship with a scattering of candles struggling to combat the gloom, and at first he didn't see the solitary hunched figure on one of the plain wooden benches at the front, another old woman in the customary black, deep in her devotions.

Pointing towards a massive oil painting above the altar,

Pepe loudly announced, "The Crucifixion, Senor Johnnie," and turning her covered head, the female worshipper glared at them.

"Come, let's leave the senora to her prayers," said Johnnie. "But before we go, why don't you ask her if she knows where Senora Adriana might be found."

Going back out into the sunlight again and waiting there for what seemed like an inordinately long time, finally, he saw Pepe emerge, but looking decidedly shifty now.

"Well, did you have any luck?"

"Si, but the senora says it would be pointless to go there."

"Still, she gave you an address. Right?"

"Si, but then if the house is empty . . ."

"But we don't know that, do we?"

He was like a dog with a bone now, for it was clear Pepe was keeping something back from him.

"So, how far exactly, is it? The actual house, I mean."

"Not far."

"Okay, then, so let's go."

But the kid still held back.

"I don't think it's a good idea for us to do this. People will talk, senor."

"About me?"

"No, Senor Johnnie, the senora. I know these people."

"Which is why I chose *you*, Pepe. You. Listen, if there's no one home we'll call it a day, okay?"

The narrow street Pepe now led him down wasn't much different from all the rest they'd already ventured along, just as empty and deathly still, with Johnnie wondering where all these so-called vigilant neighbours the kid was so worried about were hiding themselves.

Still, finally, it looked as if they might have hit paydirt, Pepe pointing out a house with an extra storey unlike the others in the street, although the ground floor windows had the usual Spanish security bars in place. Behind all that heavy curlicued iron-work the curtains were tightly drawn, possibly to keep the sunlight out, but perhaps not.

The kid seemed to be waiting for him to make some kind of a move, but what if she actually showed herself, what in God's name would he *say* to her?

"Look, maybe she might not even remember me. It might be better if you were to break the ice first."

For a moment Pepe stared at him. Then, going up to the door, leaning in close, in a firm voice, he said, "Senora Adriana? It's Pepe, Pepe from the hotel … Senora Adriana, are you in there?"

Three times in all he repeated his request, house and owner hugging their secret close like all those others in that silent, sleeping Spanish street.

"Perhaps another time, Senor Johnnie?"

"No, we're done here, I've seen enough," he told him, meaning it, too.

"Senor Johnnie, now that we're here, would you care to see our Mount of Calvario?"

"Okay, why the heck not?"

Even so, before moving on, he couldn't help directing one final glance back at number fifteen Calle El Capitano, his gaze travelling up to its roof and that one small window there, where, for the briefest of moments, he almost convinced himself he saw the curtains twitch. Of course, more than likely, it was nothing more than the reflected glare of the sun, or possibly even a cat stirring inside, end of story, just as he'd told his young guide now leading him towards the highest point of the barrio and the grotto cut from the rock there.

While Pepe prattled away about the shrine and some old hermit dude who'd made his retreat up here, *he* was taking in the view out over the terracotta-tiled roofs of the pueblo across the campo to the coast and the sea glittering there like creased silver foil in the sun, and after Pepe had run out of verbal steam they set off back down the hill again.

Coming to the bar where they'd had that beer earlier Johnnie saw that their driver was standing alongside the car now chatting companionably away with the two civil guards. Coming closer, however, it seemed that any conversation they might be having was more official than first appeared, the driver twisting his cap in his hand and with his head lowered.

"What you think they want?" he said to Pepe, who gave him a nervous grin.

"It's the way they are, Senor Johnnie, always prying, looking into other peoples' business."

"Well, not *mine,* they sure as hell don't."

Walking on, when he and the kid got much nearer, the two guards lazily turned their heads, the tall skinny one with the prominent Adam's apple staring Johnnie out, while the driver kept his gaze fixed firmly on the ground at his feet.

"Buenas tardes, senores," said Pepe cheerfully greeting the pair, whereas Johnnie made straight for the car, and after Pepe and the driver had climbed in themselves he still felt in no mood for conversation.

However, after travelling some way back down the twisting road to the coast again, he began quizzing Pepe about the two guards, and when the kid said they'd only been enquiring about their mode of transport, it was plain he was lying.

"And did you tell them why you and I came up here today?"

Even though the kid's back was turned to him he could still sense the unease coming off him in waves.

"I mean, weren't they curious?"

"Curious, senor?"

"Yeah, that's right, curious. Why this place in particular. The barrio."

"To visit the church and see the hermit's grotto, senor."

"No, goddamn it, the senora. Senora Adriana."

But it was the driver who reacted, glancing sideways at the kid as though the very mention of the name was a cause for concern, and so deciding two against one was going to get him nowhere fast, Johnnie said, "But hey, *no importante.* Just make sure Don Gustavo gets to hear one of his guests saw something of the real Spain today and he's real grateful."

Swinging around in his seat, relief written all over his young face, the kid beamed.

"You mean that, Senor Johnnie? And might *you* also tell him so yourself?"

"Why not, it's the very least I can do," he told him, while thinking, *who's the bullshitter here now,* and when they got to the hotel he handed over a generous tip to the driver and after the mini-limo had driven off he and the kid watched it disappear up the street.

"Whaddya say we take ourselves a stroll down by the playa before going inside? It's always a lot cooler there this time of day."

Still, despite Pepe being so keen on being seen in the company of his famous Americano amigo earlier, now was different, with him dragging his feet in the sand and staring out to sea as though anxius to be indoors. But no way was he getting off the hook, and so the grilling began, gently at first, then gradually more probing.

"Just seems a pity we didn't get to meet your neighbour after driving up all that way today."

"Neighbour, senor?"

"Yeah, that's what she is, isn't she? Incidentally, what's her *full* name? I mean, is she married?"

"Si, but her *esposo es muerte.*"

"But you *knew* him?"

"No, it was before I was born."

"But others *did?*"

"Si. They remember everything there, that's the way they are."

"Tell me, was it because of him she was let go from the hotel?"

Even though it was a stab in the dark, the look on the kid's face told him he might have hit the jackpot.

"Come on, Pepe, it's you and me here just talking, right? Something from the past, was it? I mean, before she arrived at the Miramar?"

Gazing out to sea, Pepe took a breath. Then he said, "People say the senora was unlucky because people remember things about him they still have a problem with."

"His politics?"

"Si, when he was mayor of the pueblo. Then later when he went off to fight in the war."

"And after he came back as well?"

"No. They say he was killed."

"Leaving her a widow like so many others."

"That's what the old people say, that's if they talk about it."

"But not a lot, right?"

The kid looked quite seriously depressed now as though he'd said far more than he should, so Johnnie told him, "But, hey, that's all in the past where it belongs, right? *Your* future's here, knockin' 'em dead on that scooter you were telling me about. Incidentally, how much to lay your hands on one of those Italian beauties anyway? Coupla large ones? Three? Four?"

Incredibly in that instant he was actually considering producing his billfold, just another big-mouth *americano* flashing his *dinero* about, before the kid told him he was in no rush to put down a *deposito* on such a machine for the wait would be worth it just to come riding back on two wheels instead of by bus or even on foot like everyone else in the barrio.

What Pepe was giving him was a much-needed history lesson, and taking it on board, he told him, "But, hey, enough of all of that. Why don't you head back inside and tell your boss about our trip today and how this *gringo* here got to learn a lot of interesting stuff he never knew before."

And to do him credit, the kid grinned.

"Me, too, Senor Johnnie. *Mi tambien.*"

Standing here by himself, it seemed that the mystery of the equally mysterious senora of the night had finally been put to rest, and here where their first encounter had taken place, even if the gap in between and waking up in bed the next day still

177

remained a blank. But then there'd been similar black holes of that kind before, reminding him he'd only had one lousy beer all day, and after watching the sea change colour for a while he strolled back up the beach to the hotel where Jorge already had that first highball waiting for him.

EUGENE

Opening his mail-box this morning he found a solitary envelope inside, a sheet of the Miramar's headed notepaper enclosed inviting him to a private function to mark the imminent departure of the hotel's celebrated Americano resident Senor Ray. Not having seen him recently, not in fact since the night they'd drank here together in Las Golondrinas, he wasn't sure what to do about it.

However, as the date and time drew nearer, anything seemed preferable to brooding up here on his own over someone whose past presence seemed still to permeate the place and him sniffing the contents of his bedroom bureau for lingering traces of her scent.

Finally, when the night arrived he took down the suit hanging in the wardrobe despite it reminding him of his own foolishness.

Showering, shaving, and putting on one of the white shirts

she'd washed and even ironed for him before she left, then the suit itself, he studied the finished effect in the mirror, regretting she no longer was able to appreciate his new image, although any relationship he might have hoped for there had been doomed from the start.

On the short walk to the Miramar he could see its neon-lit outline ahead, while beyond its perimeter the rest of rural Spain seemed to lie in darkness. Out there, it struck him, brooded something unpredictable, possibly dangerous, as well, resentful of all that opulence, making him think of the woman off somewhere in that same blackness herself, looking down on these same lights from her hilltop pueblo.

On the hotel's gravelled forecourt there seemed to be parked a far greater number of cars than usual, all expensive, making him wonder if their owners had received the same invitation as himself. At least on this occasion he happened to be correctly turned out to mix with such *senoritos,* mounting the front steps he could hear the tinkling of a piano inside coming from the Hollywood Room.

Edging his way into the crowded lounge he saw that the guest of honour himself was at its keyboard. Around him were gathered a cross-section of the usual local big-wigs and their dolled-up wives and fancy women, instantly making Furlong feel stranded between this swanky crew and a small contingent of the hotel's own staff who'd been shunted off to the rear, all standing stiff and frozen listening to the Yank at the baby grand.

When the number finished the assembled guests started

circulating once more, greeting one another with those little Spanish *besos* on alternate cheeks, a practice Furlong still couldn't carry off even if he'd wanted to, until it looked as if Don Gustavo was poised to make a speech.

Clapping his hands, waiting for the noise to die down, after a cough he began.

"Senoras, senores, honoured guests, regrettably this little gathering of ours this evening is also something of a sad occasion for the Hotel Miramar, as our famous American visitor is leaving us after his much too brief stay here. Many of you, I know, were hoping he might sing for us tonight, but unfortunately he's informed me he must protect his voice for his forthcoming concert in Madrid. However, as we've all just heard, he's been more than generous, playing for us instead. And so now, as a parting gesture of our regard for such an illustrious and favoured guest, allow me to present you, Senor Ray, with this photographic *memento* of your time spent here with us."

He motioned one of the waiters to come forward bearing something wrapped in yellow and red like the national flag flying out front, and after being revealed, Furlong saw it was a framed likeness of the singer, like the others decorating the walls, Don Gustavo reaching up to hang this latest addition midway between that of Frank Sinatra and the shaven-headed Yul Brynner.

"I'm pleased to see you've decided to honour us with your presence, even if it is only to say farewell to your famous Americano amigo".

Turning, Furlong saw it was Delgado, that police captain buddy of Guzman's.

181

"Now that we're together like this it gives me a chance to thank you both for re-directing our attention to a past case we've decided now to reopen."

Seeing the look of concern on his face, the cop laughed.

"But why don't we talk about it later at the bar just like we used to do."

After he'd moved back into the crowd again, Furlong felt himself sweat. It was as if something had been left ticking, and what made it more explosive was he saw Delgado had caught up with Guzman, the pair of them deep in conversation, until, more worrying still, Guzman directed a sly, knowing grin across the room in his direction.

Leaning over the bar and breaking into his thoughts, Jorge remarked, "Senor Ray will be greatly missed when he leaves us."

"Perhaps not by everyone."

"Si, Senor Eugene, for certain people still judge others by their own way of thinking."

In that moment it felt good to be with someone he trusted, until Don Gustavo came across ordering the kid to open more champagne, and noting the whiskey in Furlong's hand, he said, "I see Jorge here's been taking care of you. But then, like Senor Ray, you, also, have become a favoured guest of the Miramar's."

Moving closer, he murmured, "Forgive me referring to a private matter, but has your recent arrangement with the Senora Adriana proved satisfactory?"

"It seems to be working out."

"*Bueno*, I'm pleased to hear it. When the senora came seeking my advice I was happy to assist her to secure alternative employment, especially someone like her with her unfortunate history."

Having delivered his obligatory dose of poison, with a brisk shaking of the hands, Don Gustavo, as he always insisted on being addressed, slipped back into the crowd once more.

After that events seemed to take on a volition of their own, for when he next looked around, most of the people there seemed now to have left. Even Don Gustavo had disappeared, leaving the guest of honour marooned over on a far corner banquette with Delgado and Guzman just then returning from the *servicios* with that lopsided lurch of his, only more pronounced than usual alerting Furlong he might now be seriously drunk, even more disturbing, making his way straight towards him.

"Has no one ever told you drinking on your own's not only unhealthy but an insult to the company as well? Here, Jorge, give my Irish amigo whatever's he's having and make sure it's a *doble*."

Covering the mouth of his glass, Furlong told him, "Thanks, but I think I've had more than my fair share this evening."

"Come, one for the road as you and your Americano friend like to say before he flies off and forgets all about us poor people left behind here on the costa."

Incredibly enough, there seemed something close to an actual tear in his eye.

"But never mind that, the captain over there would like to talk to the pair of you about something *muy importante*," ordering Jorge, "Take Senor Furlong's drink to our table with a fresh one for Senor Ray and a bottle of your best *conac* for Capitan Delgado and myself."

Crossing the floor with him Furlong felt like he was seeing them both through Jorge's eyes, each limping in his own fashion, yet somehow, it might, appear mimicking one another, and when he got to the table, Johnnie seemed also to have a double, sitting under his own likeness on the wall behind him and staring listlessly into space unlike Delgado who seemed brimming over with affability.

"Caballeros, amigos, now we're together like this permit me to express my gratitude for drawing our attention to a matter which, quite literally, we believed dead and buried."

However, unable to contain himself, Guzman broke in, "But about to be dug up from the grave just like the accused himself!" Delgado slapping him down with, "Only three people present here are involved in this matter and the longer it stays that way the better for all concerned."

Although it was good hearing Guzman put in his place like this, Furlong still felt wary, confused, too, the mists only clearing when Delgado resumed, "None the less, fate sometimes has a habit of catching up with certain individuals when they least expect it, even someone safe as they thought holed up in their pueblo."

"Especially when that same fate comes hammering on their own front door."

But instead of chastising Guzman a second time, the police captain poured both of them shots of *conac*.

"Would it be too much to enquire who this particular "someone" under discussion happens to be here?" asked Johnnie, and with a wave of his hand Delgado gave Guzman leave to explain.

"Let's just say a certain female you and Senor Furlong here have both been in contact with, leading to Captain Delgado to become interested himself, although not for the same reasons as yourselves."

Feeling even more at sea now, for what had the singer got to do with all of this, Furlong stared down at his glass, until putting down his own drink, suddenly Johnnie erupted.

"How about we skip all this pussy-footing around and cut to the chase here!"

Spreading his hands wide in a peace-making gesture, the policeman laughed.

"Amigos, amigos, no-one is blaming you for your involvement with this person, but then if it hadn't been for that we mightn't have taken the decision to place her under surveillance when we did."

"And that includes myself and my Irish friend as well, does it?"

"Senor Ray, as a distinguished visitor to our country, while you are here it is our duty to shield you from those who continue to pose a threat to our own national security. Senor Furlong, on the other hand, as a permanent resident, should have been aware of such risks. But come let us forget such boring official matters and celebrate instead what we've really all come here for this evening."

Having none of it, however, the American was up on his feet, flushed in the face, swaying.

"Well, it might be the done thing in your own country here, but nobody, buster, *nobody* puts a tail on Johnnie Ray, home or abroad. Still, as I aim to be flyin' outa here tomorrow anyway, I guess it don't matter much. So, wishing you all the luck in the world with that sneaky little undercover operation of yours, adios and hasta la vistas, muchachas."

After he'd gone, weaving unsteadily towards the exit, Delgado turned to study the black and white portrait of the singer behind him on the back wall.

"Someone, I think, once said a picture never lies, only in this case as we've just discovered it can and often does. But then, I suppose, we should be grateful to our Americano friend for visiting our senora in her barrio and so leading us to place her and her house under observation there."

"He *went* there?"

The query had sprung from Furlong's lips before time to properly think it through, and Delgado smiled.

"On that one occasion only, but more than enough to put a close watch on the premises."

"And did this "close watch" of yours produce anything of interest?"

"Oh, much more than we ever could have hoped for. Specifically the whereabouts of someone we thought we'd never lay hands on again. At least not in this world anyway."

"But she'd been up there in plain sight all along."

The pair were studying him now with an expression midway between pity and contempt, before it was Guzman's turn to re-enter the conversation.

"*Irlandes*, once I warned you not to get involved with this *persona* as it might lead to trouble, and now it has. But then the same *puta* has guarded her secret well over the years, just like the deceitful, devious, lying *rojo* bitch she is and always has been. Still, I trust you at least managed to bed her despite Senor Ray getting his own *pene* in there first."

However, even for Delgado this felt he'd overstepped the mark.

"Amigo, I suggest it's time to take your leave of us before you regret anything further you might have to say at this time."

Appearing to crumple before them, then finally bowing with a shaming little dip of the head, Guzman said. "My sincerest apologies if I may have caused embarrassment to either one of you senores. *Buenas noches.*"

After he'd made his exit, swaying back and forth, sighing, Delgado remarked, "I'm afraid, in addition to his manners, Senor Guzman also sometimes forgets his privileged position with us here instead of where he first came from, the same barrio, in fact, as the two suspects we've previously been discussing."

"*Two*, you say?"

" Si, and now we're simply waiting for the right moment to apprehend both."

"And this second person, you know who it is?"

"A certain individual and no other. But none of that concern you. Take my advice, amigo, and forget you ever met with this troublesome senora and leave us to deal with her and the person she's been protecting up to now."

"So what will happen to them?"

"Let's say, the Caudillo has a long memory when it comes to dealing with those who once were his enemies."

"Her, as well?"

Delgado smiled.

"Not all of us are as vindictive as our American friend would seem to believe. Some of us have distanced ourselves from the past and now can be more forgiving of old foes."

"But not Guzman."

"Unfortunately, Senor Guzman still harbours old grudges formed in the barrio which have never really left him, and which is why I intend denying him any further involvement in this matter."

After touching glasses and sipping their drink, they sat there, until, yawning, Furlong climbed to his feet.

"About time to call it a day, I reckon."

"Still I hope you and I might meet up here again in more pleasant circumstances after this unfortunate business has been put to bed."

He laughed.

"And on that rather delicate note, I propose we both say *buenas noches.*"

Leaving him to finish his brandy, Furlong walked off, and reaching Reception where the night porter was on duty, he asked him, "Has Senor Ray gone up to his room?"

Anselmo, or was it Esteban, he never could remember which, blinked nervously.

"Senor Ray?"

"Si, the Americano guest."

"The senor's key is still here. I think he may have gone outside."

"You're certain of that?"

Fearing his job might be on the line, Anselmo was beginning to sweat, so Furlong told him, *"no es importante,"* moving towards the big plate glass entrance doors.

Outside on the hotel's front steps he stood for a moment breathing in the heavy, flower-scented air. Stars, way too many to begin to list, or identify even, pricked the night sky, causing him to think of *her* again somewhere under that same dark canopy. But after everything he'd learned this night any sentiment he might have had in that area had left him, something now closer to anger taking hold at being made a fool of like one of those deluded old bachelors he remembered people making fun of back home.

Taking the path leading to the beach and keeping on until he felt sand under his feet, ahead of him now he could make out the solitary figure standing gazing out to sea there, and coming closer saw him turn around to confront him with that same look of anger on his face as he'd witnessed in the bar earlier.

"Just where do those two dago creeps back there get off giving us the gestapo treatment like that? Practically accused *you* of some sorta crime against the state too. Well, didn't they, didn't they?"

Then, in an abrupt switching of tone, he said, "Still, who gives a rat's ass anyway? Let's you and me have ourselves a proper nightcap some place else, Irish. How about that Howie guy's joint? So whaddya say?"

However, having no intention of sharing the other's final booze-laden night here with him, Furlong felt his own anger take over.

"Why'd you go up to her house in the barrio like Delgado said you did?"

Staring back at him out of bleary eyes, the singer was swaying now.

"Barrio? House? Kinda lost me there, big guy."

"You *know* what I'm talking about, we both do."

"We do?"

Taking a step towards him, Furlong saw the other flinch.

"What did you want with her? Tell me, I need to know!"

Losing his balance, the other folded at the knees, falling on to the sand on his back to lie spread-eagled there.

"Why don't you come down here and join me, big guy?" Furlong heard him murmur. "I mean, check out all that celestial shit up there. That's the Big Dipper, see? Over there on the right. See?"

Fully resolved to turn and walk away, Furlong saw the singer slowly start to rise, hoisting himself up on both elbows.

"Okay, okay, hold your horses, I'll come clean, scout's honour, if that's the way you want it. Still, absolutely sure you wouldn't want to hear it over a little old drink?"

Furlong shook his head, and so, sighing, the man hunkered down facing him, began his confession.

"Guess you could say it all started right here where we are on this beach right now. Not that I remembered too much about it at the time, except coming to next day relieved of certain personal items, but having no earthly idea of how or why they mighta gone missing. Still, wouldn't have been the first time, although this was different in that our friend Delgado back there was on the case pretty prontissimo arresting some sorry-assed gypsy guy who claimed a woman might also have been present, but like in some sorta Good Samaritan role. But, like I'm telling you, that part, too, was a blank, still is, except for, well."

Rolling over on his back, he paused.

"Except for what? Come on, I want to hear it!"

"Okay, well, something she might have left back in my hotel room. Something with her name on it."

"So you lied about coming across it in the street?"

"Only after I found out you mighta had some sort of thing going on there, and I didn't want you getting the wrong idea."

"But why go up to the pueblo, her barrio?"

"Just curiosity, I guess. To put a face to the name on that medal of hers."

"And did you?"

"No. Which probably was the best outcome for all concerned."

"But not for her, not for her."

"Yeah, I guess you're right, sorry about that. Which, I suppose, leaves us back where it all started, here at the scene of the crime, you might say."

However, having heard more than enough, Furlong's waiting bed beckoned, but before he could make a move, the singer said, "Did *you* know she had someone up there with her all the time?"

"No," he lied, "I didn't. Anyway, that's got nothing to do with either one of us any more."

"Ancient history catching up, you mean?"

"That's right. Water under the bridge."

"Amen to that. Still, it's been real nice knowing you, Irish. You take care of yourself now, you hear?"

"And you, too, Yank. You, too."

Walking back to the hotel, Furlong thought he could recognise a constellation in the sky they used to call The Plough, the North Star at its tip, which helped you get your bearings on one of those pitch black Leitrim nights at home. Seeing it now out here like this, he had this sudden pang of home-sickness, just like the man he'd left still star-gazing behind him back there by himself, both of them a long way from home, although that was a word and a place that was only a fading memory now.

Ahead of him the spot-lit hulk of the hotel rose up from the sand like some great beached liner. Soon others just like it would be here on this stretch of coast too, while all those inland in small dark rooms behind white-washed walls could only watch as change came creeping towards them.

ADRIANA

Even though there's no longer any need to leave the house at this hour she still finds herself listening out for the old man and his burro making their slow way along the street below towards the Calvario Rock at the far end of the barrio. But no clip-clopping of hooves comes drifting up to her today, and wondering why she lifts her head from the pillow.

Alerted by a far less innocent sound now, someone clearing their throat, then a definite male cough, creeping out of bed to the window and looking down she can see no-one. Yet she still feels worried and climbing up to Diego's retreat under the eaves she gazes across at her neighbour's house opposite, then beyond that over the other roofs in the pueblo as far as the sierra itself already showing that first slow deepening of rose.

Standing there barefoot in the dark, her breath catches in her throat, for in the shadows below flares a single pin-prick of red followed by a second alongside reminding her of another night when another two watchers stood smoking on the outskirts of the pueblo, only this time they're outlined against a wall at the end of her street.

Still, what if they're only breaking the tedium of a night patrol with a *cigarrillo* before moving on? For an instant she's almost reassured until other figures start appearing, also in uniform, someone stepping out from the rest, his stiff bearing and long military greatcoat marking him out as their superior.

He has his head turned to the side, but when he swings it around she recognises that face, remembering him from the Miramar, although here on duty he seems larger somehow, deadlier as well.

Going back down to their bedroom, she lays a hand on Diego's shoulder, gently shaking him, then with more force, until, groaning, he turns over on his back, staring up at her out of bleary eyes.

"What's wrong? What's the matter? What is it?"

Reaching for his spectacles on the bedside table, he puts them on.

"What time is it, anyway?"

"Never mind that, it's unimportant. What *is*, they're down in the street getting ready to come for you."

"Who are?"

"Listen, you must do as I say. You must get up and go up to your *refugio* right now."

"Come back to bed, woman. You've been dreaming, and still haven't wakened properly."

Which is when she does something she's never ever done before, just as *he's* never lifted a hand to her either, and after her slap, seeing him look up at her defenceless in that way without his glasses, which she's knocked off, reaching down, she embraces him.

"Diego, please, *please* listen to me. At this very minute as we're speaking they're at the end of the street and this time they mean business. I saw them when I went up above."

"You went up to my..?"

"And where you must go now yourself."

"Come back to bed. Anyway, you need your rest, you've got to start out to your work soon."

However, in her head, it's already as if she's hearing banging on the front door and so this might be her last chance to own up, confess, and suddenly all the secrets, all the evasions and lies she's been harbouring inside come spilling out. The hotel, losing her position there, the threats from Guzman, the arrangement with the *irlandes*, and after she's finished, sitting up in bed, he says, "And you kept all this from me when you and I always shared everything?"

"But now everything's changed, everything except those out there no longer denied their *venganza*."

After she's said it the room goes very still. Then, throwing the bed-clothes aside, he swings both legs out, and seeing them suddenly naked like that, pale, shrunken, too, she's filled with pity for this man forced to hide himself away like a leper all these years.

"Fetch my clothes," he commands, and unable to refuse, lifting them off the back of the chair and bringing them to him she holds them out to him.

"No, no, I don't mean those. My suit. And my good shoes, as well."

"But you haven't got time for this. You must, you *have* to go up to your room above now!"

"Don't argue with me, do as I say."

Still in a fog, she goes to the wardrobe, lifting out his old black wedding two-piece there with the nipped in waist and wide lapels and watches as he dresses himself, everything a tight fit on account of him not getting any proper exercise these many long years.

"Remember the last time I wore this?" he says. "When they voted me in as mayor, even if it did make me look just like a *senorito?*"

"Why are you talking like this? Are you mad, or are you still drunk?"

"Well, if I was, no longer. *You* made certain of that."

Dropping on to the bed, she feels the tears start to flow, something she hasn't given in to for a very long time, and moved by her distress he comes and sits beside her just like the Diego of old when he was her *novio* and she was as shy and awkward then as himself.

"Listen, listen to me. Let them come and do their damnedest. To hell with them, you hear? Every last miserable one of them."

"So then you *do* believe me?"

"Haven't I always?"

"Not this time."

"Well, you must make allowances for an old man who's become set in his ways."

"Haven't I always?"

In spite of everything he smiles, the two of them sitting together just like any other barrio couple except he's wearing

196

a Sunday suit and she's in her night clothes still, and then he tells her, "You must get dressed now as well."

"But why?"

"Because you don't want to give them the satisfaction of seeing you like this."

Taking her hands in his, he says, "Look, we both of us knew this day might come, and now that it has there's nothing we can do about it now that they're certain I'm here."

"Certain? But how?"

"Because once I was careless and someone out there must have seen the curtains move."

"And you never told me?"

"Would it have made a difference now if I had?"

Rising and going over to the window again, she looks down on the street below, empty once more.

"Well? Can you see them? How many are there?" he says, and turning she looks at him sitting on the bed, dressed, not for a wedding now, but a funeral, it strikes her.

"Put on your day clothes, the ones you wear to the hotel."

But realising what he has in mind, she protests, "No, no, I'm not leaving you up there all alone in your coffin."

"Which is what it often felt like, believe me … But there's no longer time for any of that, do as I tell you."

Reaching into the wardrobe, she brings out, not her hotel uniform as requested, but an old-fashioned, high-bodiced costume with long sleeves, like his suit something she hasn't worn since they once led lives like other people. Closing her eyes, holding it against her cheek, she almost imagines it still retains the scent of the mimosa spray she carried on her wedding day.

In the corner of their bedroom there's a pierced wooden

screen, and going in behind it and changing out of her night-dress there, she puts on the only formal garment she's ever possessed. But because of all her long daily journeys down through the campo to the costa and back the frock hangs loose on her, and emerging, she nervously waits for his reaction, and at first he stares at her. Then his face changes in a smile.

"It seems I've forgotten just how *bonita* my wife still is. If people could see us like this they'd take me for your father."

However, while they've been talking the world outside has moved on at its own pace with all those other sounds now heralding the start of another new day. Dogs barking, burros braying, humans, as well, a low, swelling murmur of voices growing stronger, and Diego calling out, "What's happening? Can you see them?"

"No, but I can hear them."

Then, making one final despairing effort, she pleads, "What if *I* went down and showed myself, it might put them off the scent."

"Who needs to get wind of their quarry when the prey's already been sighted?"

"So you've become some sort of human fox or rabbit now, have you?"

"Or mole, a *topo*? Isn't that the name they have for people people hiding themselves away in the dark like this?"

"While *I* went out every day struggling to keep the wolf from the door and put food on the table."

Unable to keep her bitterness at bay, she watches him bow his head, and seeing him like that, she feels shame, pity, too, like a mother might have for a child refusing, or more like, incapable, of growing up, which has been his punishment

198

while she's been free to enjoy the changing seasons and the fresh sea air as once they did as a couple.

"No," she says, "why give them the satisfaction of breaking down the door and seeing us like this. Let's face them together, like when you flushed out their rich friends and they were the ones cowering in their holes."

After a moment he nods. Then, "So, tell me, what do you think?"

"What do you mean?"

Spreading his hands, smiling, he says, "Like this. How do I look?"

And in that instant, despite all the years and the present trouble, she still sees in front of her the one she first fell in love with.

"Well?"

"Como uno caballero autentico."

"Truly?"

"Truly. A real man ... Now, are we ready? Shall we go?"

SILVER'S CITY

One of the seminal novels of Northern Irish literature

Silver Steele is a legend, the man who fired the first shot of the Troubles, with his name painted on walls all over his city, Belfast.

When Galloway, a younger paramilitary, frees Silver from prison Silver discovers that he is now a symbol, "a ready-made martyr," for a cause he no longer believes in.

In a city at war the two engage in a duel to the death.